The Dengu Odyssey

By Cheryl Castro

Published by
Eagle's Wings Publishing
Medford, Oregon

2010 ©Cheryl Castro

Cover Illustration by Emily Burdge

ISBN -10: 0981936261
ISBN -13: 978-0-9819362-6-0

The Dengu Odyssey

By Cheryl Castro

ACKNOWLEDGMENTS

I thank two of my friends, Nancy Olson and Elda Lee Carnes. They reside in the beautiful forestlands of Trail, Oregon. Both are schoolteachers, and helped me with the first and roughest editing. They have taught me so much about using the English language, and the rules that apply to it. God bless you both.

Also, I thank my Lord Jesus who has entrusted me to write these tales of Uri and his friends.

Table of Contents

Forward

It was a year and a half since that fateful night the men from the Dombara tribe came across the Green Sea in large boats to capture Uri, and all the children living in the Pinola village. Fourteen years before that capture, the Pinola tribe, realizing they could no longer produce offspring, raided the Dombara people several times, kidnapping infants, and raising them as their own. Suddenly the Dombara people took back what was theirs, and the Pinola tribe had no children and no hope of a future.

Uri wanted to leave Dombara Land and go home. He didn't want to stay in the in the land with parents and siblings he didn't know. However, these people introduced him to a new faith. They believed in The Creator of All, but Uri only knew about the evil spirits that resided in his homeland, and didn't want anything to do with their beliefs.

Uri and Rill, his compatriot and adversary, escaped in a stolen boat. While at sea, a storm took Rill's life, but Uri managed to wash up on a sand bar, and began slowly dying of dehydration. Because of a vision, his cousin, Coran, a priest of this Dombara faith, knew what had happened and rescued Uri. That was when Uri accepted The Creator of All and His Son. That was when he returned to the Pinola tribe, his adopted family, and began to spread the Good News.

Things did not go smoothly. A man named Zekod and his two sons began to deviously persecute not only Uri, but also all the new believers. Zekod feared the new faith would

1

destroy the belief in the spirits he used to gain power and profit. Many of the Pinolas came to him for potions and charms to ward off certain evils that befell their families or crops. If the new belief grew, he would stand to lose not only wealth, but power as well. Being a clever and cunning man, he knew he must work undercover.

Persecution grew, not only in the number of incidents, but now in severity as well. Uri and his small group must find the strength. He must be brave enough to find a way to prove that Zekod and the others were behind these cruel and evil acts.

Map of Pinola and Dombara

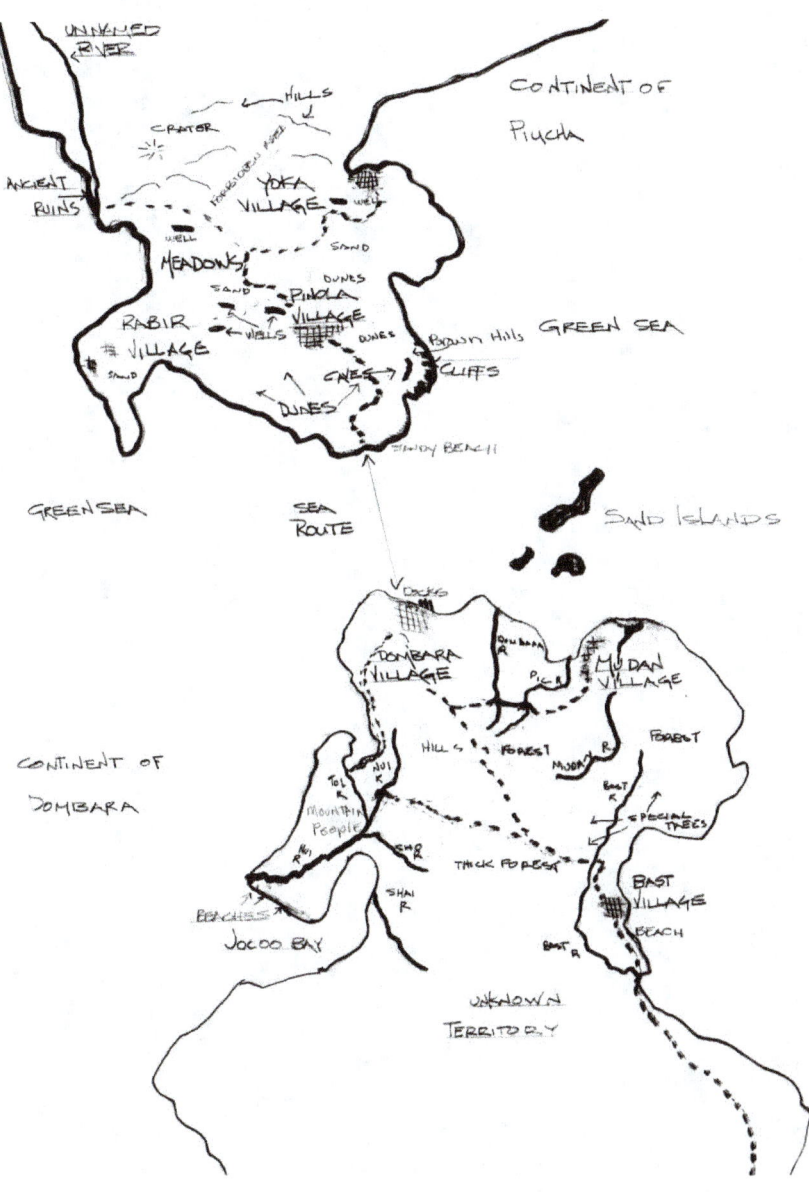

Chapter One

Pinola Land

Uri sat on the sand close to the water, watching as the waves slapped the shoreline. His only thoughts were on Tofini, his friend who back in the village lay dying. Coran, his cousin, was late. Uri hoped Coran had received the message about Tofini before he left Dombara Land.

More Dombara families had crossed the sea, like sister Tika and her new husband Koori, to help with the converts. A need to communicate became evident. A Dombara sailor volunteered to deliver letters and packages three times a week, for a fee. As a result of this communication, the Pinola and Dombara tribes grew closer together.

Uri felt a foreboding in his spirit, so he was thankful he was able to send the message to Coran, because Tofini was new to The Way and a prime target for their enemies.

At last, Uri saw a sail in the distance. Within minutes, Coran stepped out of the boat and tied it next to several others moored near the shore.

Uri went to embrace his cousin. "It's good to see you."

"Yes, it has been too long." Coran answered.

"Did you get the message about Tofini?"

5

"Yes I did. I know what happened to him. The symptoms are typical of a poison used by the Bast people." Coran looked to the box he brought with him.

"What?" Uri stopped, and looked intently at Coran as he removed the robe that identified him as a Dombara priest and healer. The sun in Pinola Land was much hotter than in the green, lush Dombara Land. He folded up the robe and carried it under his arm.

"He was poisoned." Coran explained.

Uri had never seen the box Coran had brought with him. "What is in that box?"

"It contains a tube with the poison I think was used on Tofini. It is tasteless, and can be put a in drink or on food. No one would know. I need it to make the antidote."

"Where did you get it?" Uri was amazed.

"It is better if you don't know." Coran said, looking in front of him as they walked along the path.

Uri frowned. What was the secret he was better off not knowing about?

Coran walked ahead, not looking back at Uri. "Let's go straight to Tofini's home. I want to look at him and make sure I am correct in my diagnosis."

"Aren't you hungry? Beka is making breakfast cakes for us." Uri said.

"Your sister's cakes make my mouth water. However, first things first."

Tofini's hut was close, and when they entered, Uri saw his friend resting on a large pillow in the front room of the hut. He was pale and weak, but better than when Uri saw him yesterday.

6

"How are you feeling?" Coran asked as he looked into Tofini's eyes and checked his heartbeat.

"Better, but I am still having spells of terrible pain and I am having frightening dreams."

Tofini's mother stood in the doorway to the kitchen. "They are more than dreams. They come during the day or night, and he screams about monsters and demons."

"Yes," said Coran, "Those are hallucinations. They will eventually fade away. I will have an antidote for the pain in a couple of days. Do you think you can hang on until then?"

"I have no choice." Tofini said weakly.

"Did you eat or drink anything different than usual in the last few days?" Coran asked.

"I don't know." Tofini whispered.

"We were at the marketplace two days ago." His mother said. "I saw a stranger offer him a piece of fruit."

"Did you eat it?" Coran leaned forward.

"Yes, I remember now. I did take a bite, but I didn't like it, so I gave it back to him."

"You are fortunate only to have taken one bite." Coran said grimly. "It will take two days to brew the antidote. Until I return, drink plenty of kavac milk." He referred to the common animal most people keep for their rich milk. Coran looked to Tofini's mother. "He needs to drink as much as you can get down him. If he throws it up, give him more."

They hurried from Tofini's hut into the Pinola village. Things were quiet today and they arrived at Uri's small, comfortable hut in record time. However, instead of the smell of breakfast, Uri smelled trouble. Denar and Abosol waited for them in the front room.

"What is it?" Uri asked with a hushed voice.

"Kwoll is very ill." Denar replied. "One of the newest converts, he is the son-in-law of Pattis, the head of the Council."

"What is wrong with him?" Coran asked.

"It came on him sudden, after last night's dinner." Abosol said. "He began having terrible pains in his muscles. Then he lapsed into an unconscious state, and began hallucinating."

"Another one?" Uri said. "This is truly alarming."

A frown passed over Coran's face. "Take me to him."

The group headed down a path, and within a few minutes were at the doorway of Kwoll's hut. They entered, and his wife Lilla greeted them, ringing her hands. "He seems much worse. He is bellowing in pain."

Coran went alone into the room where Kwoll lay on his sleeping mat. Uri glanced through the open door at the man, his face covered in perspiration, and his legs drawn up to his belly.

Coran came back out. "He has been poisoned the same way. Tell me what he ate last night."

"Only some vegetables we bought at the marketplace yesterday." Lilla answered.

"Did you wash them first?"

She looked at the floor. "No, it was late and I made his dinner in a hurry."

"You didn't eat?" Coran asked.

"No. I ate some roasted kavac at the marketplace. I wasn't hungry."

Coran left Lilla with the same instructions about the milk.

They left and walked into the harsh sunshine.

"I have to make the antidote as soon as possible." Coran said.

"It seems it is coming from the marketplace." Uri spoke first. "Tofini said a stranger gave him fruit to eat."

"That was the way they received the poison." Coran explained. "It comes from the Bast people. The question is... how did it get over here? This deadly poison comes from boiling twigs from a bitter tree called the Meechu. It doesn't grow on this side of the Green Sea. It's indigenous to the area near the Bast Tribe."

"Where is that?" Denar asked Coran.

"South of the Dombara Land."

"Do you think the stranger was Bast?" Uri questioned.

"No. They are so very different... a Bast would stand out. I think it was someone from a tribe around here." Coran said.

Uri stopped and raised his eyebrows. "The Bast would find someone to do the job for a Pinola."

Denar and Abosol looked blankly at each other so Uri spoke again.

"The Bast found someone to do the job for Zekod."

"We can't prove that." Denar said.

"No, but it makes the most sense." Uri defended the idea. "Zekod has tried to stop us from the very beginning."

"Why Kwoll and Tofini?" Abosol asked. "To see them suffering saddens my spirit. At the same time, I want to punish

9

whoever did this. I like Kwoll, and being a new believer myself, we spent a lot of time together studying the New Way."

"That's easy to answer." Coran said. "First, Kwoll's family is important to the village. Second, they both became followers recently. They must have been in the wrong place at the wrong time."

"Someone is trying to make a point." Denar said grimly.

"Yeh, someone." Uri said with a sullen tone in his voice.

They made their way back to Uri's home. The weather had turned hot. The smell of blowplant, a common weed that crawled along the ground, rooting everywhere, was prevalent. The heavy, musky scent wasn't unpleasant, just strong, and it irritated Uri, adding to the uneasiness that enveloped him.

"If Zekod and his sons are the guilty ones, we need to find a way to prove it." Abosol said, then stopped on the path and turned west so he could feel the breeze on his face. "The Bast must have come across the sea to meet with the men. I wonder if we can find footprints leading from the village west, to the sea."

Coran looked puzzled. "How can you discern prints in the village, there must be hundreds around?"

"Not in the north where the village ends and the trails go up into the hills. The forbidden areas are up there. No one goes there. If we find footprints there it would mean someone is secretly traveling north." Abosol explained.

"That makes sense. They couldn't go down to the caves and beach area, because there is traffic in that direction. They had to find a way to the western shore." Denar nodded.

"Good," chimed in Uri. "Let's head that way today, and see what we can find."

Chapter Two

The Antidote

When they reached Uri's hut, breakfast was cold. Beka, disappointed, whipped about the kitchen mumbling.

"Sorry Beka," Uri explained. "There has been a very bad situation in the village."

"There have been poisonings among the village people." Denar added.

"Oh," Beka stopped in the middle of her kitchen. "How did this happen?"

"Please, don't eat anything from the market until we figure this out." Uri warned.

She looked at Suwat and put her hand over her mouth, stunned.

"Since you have a permanent stall at the marketplace," Coran asked Beka, as they sat down at the table, "Did you notice a stranger, or someone you didn't recognize wandering around the last few days?"

"No one." She answered in a hushed voice.

As they ate the cold food, plans began to form for the day.

First Coran had to start making the antidote. He brought only a small amount of the poison with him from Dombara Land. Everyone sat in the living area, and Coran opened the wooden box he brought with him. It was small, rectangular, and shallow. There were strange characters carved on the top. Uri studied it, but was unable to make out what they were.

Coran showed them a small tube. It was wider at the top, and then narrowed down at the bottom. In it was four drops of the poison.

Coran reached out with the tube to Denar. "Spit in it."

Denar looked startled.

"This is how we make the antidote. Exactly three men spit in the tube. The contents ferment in the heat for two days. Something in human saliva produces the necessary material to begin a reaction with the poison. After the time allowed, a malodorous black liquid forms. It counteracts the horrible pain, and spasms the poison produces in the muscles of the body. However, it does not help the other symptom, grotesque hallucinations. Those gradually diminish. If not treated in time, the victim will die from violent muscle contractions, or a heart attack from the hallucinations. The two other victims have survived until now, but not without serious problems. If we get to them soon it will help."

Denar, Abosol, and Suwat spit into the tube. Coran placed it in the back yard in the sun.

"While we are waiting for that to ferment, we can start to follow the trail up to the North Country." Uri said, being very eager to be on the way to catching Zekod.

Beka shook her head. "You are too young for this kind of dangerous activity."

"But Dear, he is sixteen now and considered a man." Suwat tried to reason with his wife.

"No, let the older men prowl around." she demanded.

Uri went over and held both of Beka's hands in his. "I have been through much more dangerous situations. I can handle myself." He kissed her forehead. "Besides," he added, grinning. "I'm going whether you like it or not." That brought a chuckle to everyone, including Beka.

By mid afternoon the four, Denar, Abosol, Coran, and Uri loaded up their packs with water and snacks. They left the village behind and started up the hills, looking for tracks of men going in that direction.

Abosol, a good hunter and tracker, hunched his large body down and studied the ground, while his wild, dark hair ruffled in the rising breeze. A hulk of a man, older, and widowed, he was known for his ability to track any person or animal, especially the wona, a worm that lived in the desert sand. Uri had been jealous of his abilities when he was younger, but now he admired the man. Uri danced with glee when Abosol, with fiery zeal, accepted The Creator and His Son.

"I think we are looking at three or maybe four men. I can see there are fresh tracks." Abosol pointed to several. "And these are old ones. The same type, Pinola foot bindings."

They continued up the hill, Abosol leading the way. It took about an hour to reach the top. In front of them rose The Forbidden Area. Many years ago, several talismans had been placed to warn the people of the evil spirits that occupied the land beyond. The reason was history. Years ago, the Pinola men and women took their families and went to find the fiery ball that landed from the sky. They came home ill, and some died. Then the babies stopped coming, and within a few years the Pinolas realized their tribe was doomed.

13

In order to stop people from wandering around in that direction, the council members placed warnings in the form of talisman at the top of the hills hoping it would please the Spirits and remove the curse. It didn't. However, they continued to forbid anyone to venture past the warnings.

They looked up at the tall structures, made of straw and trinkets, placed in both directions as far as they could see. X's in a line along the top of the hill. People had come here and occasionally placed trinkets for new requests. They wanted to please the Evil Spirits, or thank them for their not bringing bad times, hunger, crop failures or sickness upon them.

Uri fought the urge to tear them all down and rip them apart. This superstition was damaging his people.

"Such nonsense." Coran shook his head. "As if straw and bits of stuff could ward off evil and protect people."

"A talisman is an ancient superstition." Denar reached out and touched one. "Someday we will come up here and take them all down."

"I pray that day will come soon." Uri whispered. "Come on, let's go past this junk, and see where these footprints lead to."

"No." Denar said flatly.

"Why?" Uri frowned.

"If we go past this, without Pattis' permission, anything we find will not be accepted."

"Fine, let's go back and get permission." Uri impatiently replied.

"Slow down, my young friend. We need to talk about how to approach him. Pattis, not only is the leader of the council, he believes in the ancient superstitions." Denar said.

14

Uri watched the sun lower in the sky. "Pattis will give us permission, I know he will."

As they turned to head back down to the lower sandy desert, they discussed the many avenues of approach. Pattis was easy to talk to and was friendly with the believers, but passing into the Forbidden Area might take some special persuasion.

Soon they had retreated to the edge of the rocky hills, and Uri looked down as the setting sun flooded over the Pinola desert. The desert covered the southwestern end of the sand dunes and continued northwest as far as anyone ever dared venture.

Uri loved this time late in the afternoon, when the desert acquired a tranquil tone. The texture of the sky entered a realm of azure blue. The horizon faded away into forever and the coolness of the air crept over the sand like a soft essence.

A shrill scream startled him, and shattered it all.

Chapter Three

Murder

They ran to the vicinity of the screams as hot air undulated in front of them. A woman lay crumpled on the dry sand. Her legs were pulled up tight to her chest and her hair stringy, matted with sand and blood, covered her painfully twisted face. Every muscle was taut and quivering. Again, she screamed.

It echoed through the desert, and carried on the northeast breeze, toward the Pinola village. When they reached her, Uri gasped and pointed to an ovi feather covered with blood that was stuck in the palm of her left hand. The meaning was obvious. Someone was trying to tell them the spirits that lived in and ruled the Pinola Land were unhappy with the spread of the Good News. The feather pointed to the birds, the ovis Uri had brought with him from the Dombara Land, as the cause of their displeasure. The blood was a warning, and piercing of the left hand depicted evil. No one had ever seen this before, but they all could read the meanings. Uri believed it was typical of something Zekod would do.

This was the third case of poisoning. Where was it coming from? Uri knew that spreading fear was a convenient tool their enemies used. Fear was the only thing they had left. Lies and outright intimidations over the past year toward the growing group that gave their lives to The Creator and the Savior, had failed.

This woman lived right down the road from his home. She and her husband recently accepted the New Way. Uri remembered the way her eyes sparkled with joy and how she clasped her hands together when Coran prayed over them. Now she was hardly recognizable. Her face deathly grey and eyes bloodshot, she opened her mouth and reached up to the sky with claw-like hands.

"Why is she so far out in the desert?" Uri asked as tears clouded his eyes.

"Someone wanted us to find her out here." Denar said.

"And so she would die." Coran added.

Uri crawled over to the woman, looking from Coran to Denar.

She pleaded with her eyes. "H-help me…"

"We are trying." Coran lifted her up. "Can you tell us who did this to you?"

She looked vacantly into his face.

"Let's carry her back to the village." Abosol lifted her in his arms.

"It may be too late." Coran whispered.

Looking into a void, her pupils contracted, and she began to shake violently, "No, NO!" She screeched, and went limp.

Abosol put her back down on the sand, and Coran bent over, placing his ear to her chest. "She's dead." he whispered. "We found her too late."

Uri pounded his fists into the sand. He cried. "It's not fair, not right!"

17

"This time it is murder." Denar stood and shook with rage. His ruddy complex flamed red. "We can't let this go on any longer."

Tears spilled from Uri's eyes over his cheeks and pooled near his chin. He shook his head in frustration. "Even though we know that Zekod is probably behind it all, we have no proof."

"We will have to follow them." Denar said. "As we found today, someone is going into the forbidden area. Something is going on up there."

"Probably near the sea." Abosol added. "We are the only ones that can uncover the proof needed to show who is trying to frighten the villagers away from The Creator; the malicious men seeking to turn all against us. When the dust storms came in the fall many people said it was punishment for allowing us to teaching The Way and spreading the message of this new life."

"This will not stop until we can reveal the ones responsible for these poisonings, and this woman's death." Denar clenched his fists. "We must meet with Pattis and get permission to go back and cross over into the Forbidden Area. We must find something that will stop these fiends before someone else becomes a victim and dies."

Coran's face was a mask of sadness. "Where goodness is present, evil will rise to meet it." He whispered. He said a brief prayer, and then covered the dead body with his cloak. "She is now in the arms of our Savior."

Mournfully, they began preparing to transport her back to her home in the Pinola village.

Abosol stayed behind and began looking around the area. "I see something was dragged here. Probably the woman, but other footprints are scattered all over." He looked around for a few more minutes, finally turned and ran to catch up with his companions.

It was dark by the time they got back to the village and word got to Pattis. In order not to arouse anyone's curiosity, Pattis came to Denar's home instead of everyone going to the Meeting Hall. Even though Pattis was sympathetic to the new beliefs, Uri knew he would be reluctant to allow the group to venture past the talisman, at the forbidden north end of the land. However, his son-in-law was a victim. That may help make the decision needed.

"The young woman is dead?" Pattis asked, looking at the bundle lying in the other room.

Denar spoke softly. "Yes, we found her too late. I can't swear her death was intentional, however, I believe it was murder."

"There has never been a case of premeditated murder in our history. Kwoll is not doing well. I'm afraid..." he sighed, and then said absently. "Her name is Letura. Her husband will be coming to get her body." The stooped elderly man looked intently into Coran's eyes. "Where is the poison coming from?"

"It has to be from a tribe that lives in my land." Coran spoke up. "They live in the south, and use several kinds of poisons, mainly to kill animals. However, I do not think this type is for animals. There is no reason to torture an animal just to kill it for food. This is an evil thing."

Pattis continued. "There are other types of poison?"

"There is one they put on the tip of their spears. It has strange properties. It causes the speared animal to fall into a coma, but stay alive for weeks. This way they can capture many at one time, store them, and then kill one when they need food." Coran pulled his robe tightly around him as he spoke. "No one is sure what that poison is or where it comes from. That is one of the mysteries of the Bast people. They are very secretive and dangerous."

Pattis looked suspiciously at Coran. "How is it that you know so much about these people, and where did you get the poison for making the antidote? Lilla told me about it."

"There is a young man in our village who lived with them many years as a child. He related many secrets to us, including the poisons."

The room was dark. Shadows and light from the lamp danced on the far wall. Uri stared at the shadows as he listened to the men speak.

"Why would someone from the Pinola tribe contact or have dealings with these… these Bast people? They are so far away. It doesn't make sense." Pattis looked at Uri. "Do you have any ideas?"

"We found footprints traveling north." Uri edged in closer. He had stayed in the background, allowing the older men to deal with the elder, Pattis. "We would like to be allowed to follow them. Maybe we can identify the people from our tribe who are getting the poison, and from whom."

Pattis rubbed his hand over his face and sighed. "I believe anyone has the right to believe whatever they wish." He looked at Uri. "The believers who came from the Dombara land, your sister Tika and her husband, they have done much good here. They have assisted the elderly, and fed the poor. All of us have enjoyed the presence of their baby, little Ranui", Uri's little nephew who was only six weeks old.

The Pinolas couldn't get enough of gazing at him. The tribes, on both sides of the sea, were ecstatic when he was born. It had been a very long time since a baby had been born in the Pinola village.

Uri's mind wandered back to the spiritual ceremony of naming him. It was an ancient ritual, and took place seven days after his birth. The parents presented the baby to the Lord on the alter Koori built in the large room of his home. The lighting was low, and a cooling breeze drifted through the open doors and windows. Wearing nothing but his chooko, a soft cloth that covered his bottom, the father prayed over his son. Then he handed the baby to Coran. Coran looked into the sweet tiny face and smiled. After offering prayer, Coran kissed the baby's forehead then handed him back to Koori.

Everyone was quiet, waiting for the Lord to impress on the father's mind the ancient name, a name that implied the destiny of the child. Uri couldn't move a muscle, being enraptured with the moment. The silence grew heavy. Finally, Koori put his son on the table and was quiet. Then he smiled. "His name shall be Ranui", meaning "The happy beginning of all things." Uri heard everyone laugh and clap. Ranui it was; the beginning of hope for the Pinolas.

The next ritual would be the tattoo, performed on the baby's right heel. Uri didn't stay around for that. The thought of the little one crying as the tattoo marked the tiny foot, was more than Uri cared to deal with. He preferred to leave while everyone was happy and celebrating.

However, not everyone in the village was happy. A few men used fear of the evil spirits, to continue the old superstitious ways and rituals, for profit and power. Because instilling the good news brought truth and enlightenment these men were losing control. Belief created a freedom for the Pinolas when they accepted The Creator. They no longer allowed fear, superstitions, and rituals to rule their lives. Uri warned them all that they would meet with much opposition.

Uri stopped his mind from wandering, and concentrated on what was being said in the darkened room where they sat, waiting for Pattis' decision.

"Not everyone shares your openness, Pattis." Coran said. "There are those who want to turn the tribe against the Believers and drive them out. That way they will gain their control back."

Pattis was clearly troubled. He paced back and forth in Denar's small front room. "If we go back to the old ways, the Pinola Tribe will have no future. We must discover what is going on."

Uri smugly grinned to himself. Pattis had finally realized what Uri tried to tell him months ago.

"You believe these evil men will continue, and again, go as far as murder?" Pattis asked.

"Yes, whatever it takes. Remember, Kwoll and Tofini are still very sick." Abosol said.

Denar edged closer. "We have reason to believe there are some in the council connected to these men. Please be careful what you disclose to others."

Pattis looked up in surprise. "In the council?"

Denar spoke again, ignoring his question. "I know it is against the law to venture past the many talismans into The Forbidden Area at the north lands. However, the men who are doing this evil thing have already broken the law. If you grant us permission, we will travel north, and find where they are going to obtain the poison. That is the only way we can get proof.

"We must have proof." Abosol agreed. "Without absolute proof it is only their word against ours."

"I want this to end." Pattis nodded his head. Uri noticed how his hands trembled ever so slightly. "You must tell me who you suspect."

"We don't want to make accusations against certain people unless we are sure." Abosol said.

"Very well, you have my permission. My word overrides the council, but this must be kept between us. No one else can know, especially since there are spies among the members. Go quickly and quietly, in the cover of darkness."

Chapter Four
Beyond the Boundaries

Late in the morning, Coran went outside to check on the antidote. He brought it back in the kitchen and showed everyone.

"Look how it changed. The liquid is black. I'll extract a very small amount to administer to Kwoll and Tofini." He went to his wooden chest and showed everyone a strange looking object. "This will hold the liquid until I give it to Kwoll and Tofini. A swallow is all they need." He put on his cloak. "Let's get this done."

They went to Kwoll's hut. He looked as if he was next to death, and let out a bellow that shook Uri to his bones. He went outside and waited until Coran was finished.

"I'm afraid the hallucinations have damaged his mind." Coran said sadly. "We won't know for a few more days. At least he is out of that pain."

Uri and Coran went swiftly to Tofini's home next. There had been no improvement in the hallucinations.

"Will this make him well?" his mother asked.

"This will take away the pain. The nightmares and hallucinations will diminish with time. He is fortunate. He only took a small taste of the fruit. Are you sure you don't know who offered him the fruit?"

"No, I wasn't paying any attention."

Coran lifted the tube to Tofini's mouth, and coaxed him to swallow. "Hold your nose and swallow."

He gagged and shuddered. "That is awful."

Uri thought, *"It's a good thing you don't know what's in it."*

Denar and Abosol were waiting when Uri and Coran arrived back home.

"How did it go?" asked Denar.

"We won't know anything for a few days. I did what I could. Now it is up The Creator. He is the Almighty healer."

***

That night they set out as the sun faded behind the dunes. Uri followed Abosol and Denar, with Coran close behind. Near the village, Abosol picked up fresh footprints in the sand. It revealed three men, and because of the familiar markings of foot bindings, they knew the prints were Pinolas. The tracks moved toward the north area, past the talisman, and continued up into the hills. Now they veered to the west. Towards the sea as Abosol suspected.

Up in the hills, north of the Pinola village, the sand became rock and loose stones. While they climbed, Coran hummed softly, which lulled Uri into a positive state of mind.

Singing was new to Uri. He had never heard singing or humming until he lived in the Dombara Land. Just before he left for home there was a woman at the play field singing. She strummed an instrument on her lap that had four tight strings, and it made a sweet sound. Uri grew quite enamored by it.

25

Whenever Coran hummed, he thought of that incident, and his mood became light and happy.

"Walking up these hills isn't so tough. In fact it's fun." Uri thought. However, as they went higher, sandy rocks began to slip under their feet, and Uri had to concentrate more on keeping his balance. The four became quiet and attempted not to send rocks rolling down the hills behind them. Climbing these hills, however, sent a noisy message that alerted others that men were on the trail.

Uri was breathless by the time they reached the top. The land suddenly flattened out and Uri realized they stood silhouetted against groves of trees that littered the far landscape. *Easy to spot*, he thought. Denar motioned for all of them to lay flat on the ground. There they stayed.

The second moon sat yellow and plump on the horizon. Uri watched, while it evaporated behind the far away craggy hills. True darkness claimed the sky and land, and dropped a veil of eeriness, as it wrapped around the night. None of them had ever been this far north. They couldn't begin to guess what terrain lay ahead, or what they would discover.

They lay on the ground, motionless. As minutes stretched into hours, Uri dozed off. The fiery itching of his foot awoke him. It was agonizing, but he tried not to scratch. Then he noticed his left arm tingled. He was laying on it, but when he moved slightly he drew a frown from Abosol.

"Please, can't we get up now?" Uri begged. His foot burned, itched, and the agony was climbing up his leg.

Scanning the horizon, the big man motioned for them to rise and continue following the tracks. Grateful for the opportunity, Uri scratched his foot furiously and found tiny insects had been climbing all over him. He wiped them off and shuddered. Uri believed that if someone laid quietly long enough these tiny, crawling demons would completely overwhelm them.

They crept along, veering west following the tracks diligently. The night breeze was at their backs.

"This is not good." Abosol looked around. "We are downwind. Animals can smell us."

"We can't do anything about the weather." Uri said, with a sharp tongue.

"No cousin, only The Creator has power over the air." Coran replied. "Let us pray no animals are within the immediate area."

Uri was chagrined. He thought, *"Will I ever learn to keep my sarcastic mouth shut?"*

The horizon showed the first light. They had entered a wooded area and it took great care to find more tracks. At dawn's first light, they continued to a steep embankment.

Abosol pointed down. "We have to crawl down through the underbrush. The tracks go through here."

The group began to edge their way down. The hill was slippery, and loose rock and dirt revealed how far it was to the bottom.

Halfway down Uri felt his foot slip, then the other followed suit. He began to slide and fall, rolling over and over. He couldn't stop himself. He felt something hit him hard in the side. Then he hit his head on a branch from a tree as he rolled past. He knew the bushes were scratching his whole body. As suddenly as it started, it was over, and Uri lay stunned at the bottom of the escarpment. His outstretched hand felt wet and he looked into a shallow river of water, moving swiftly past him through the sand of a beach and into the Green Sea.

Denar and Coran were upon him immediately. "Are you all right?"

"Look at the cut on his forehead." Denar brushed Uri's hair back. "He's scratched all over."

Abosol made it to the bottom, and wet his scarf with water from the river. He laid it on Uri's head.

"I'm fine, just banged up a bit." Uri shook his head to clear it and sat up.

He pointed in front of him. "Look how the shallow river crosses the sand and flows into the sea."

They all stared past the river at the immense body of water, close to where they sat. At the shoreline, it radiated a deep turquoise. The color continued until several yards out, and then it turned green. At the horizon, the color was the deepest black-green Uri had ever seen. The sea was always that color, it never changed, even during storms.

Coran whispered, as the sun rose behind them. "Look straight across the river to the hills."

They all gasped. Caves scattered around the edge of the water gave way to cliffs with carved multi-level structures that rose into the sky. Ancient, but still intact, they filled the whole area. There were stones neatly placed so people were able to climb. From the bottom, the stones zigzagged all the way to the top of the cliff.

"Who built that?" Uri uttered with amazement.

"It had to be eons ago." Coran said.

Abosol whispered. "I wonder if they are still occupied."

At that moment, they saw a man they all could identify as a Pinola, step out of an opening, and the four trackers fell on their stomachs. In silence, they watched as three others joined the man. Uri gasped as he noticed one was Bast. He felt Coran nudge him in the side. Uri nodded. What was this all about?

They were far enough away that their features could not be discerned, yet close enough to see their clothing and some details. Then Uri lost his breath, as another figure appeared. This one had blonde hair, not in the typical braid, but cut short in Bast style, still definitely a Dombara. As the four figures exchanged words, Uri thought he heard, "Goodbye," and "Contact you soon."

The Bast and Dombara figures turned and disappeared down the back of the cliff, probably making their way to a boat. The three Pinola figures climbed up the stones and made their way over to an area where an old footbridge crossed the river. When they reached the other side, they disappeared into the area that lead back down the trail Uri and the others had followed up.

Uri was speechless. Finally, Coran found his voice. "That was revealing."

Abosol rose and pointed to the cliffs. "I suggest we climb into those dwellings and see if we find any evidence."

"We must wait. It won't be safe until the boat has left." Coran added.

They waited until the tiny silhouette of a two-man boat came into view from behind the cliffs and headed to the horizon. Coran led the way as Uri and his companions crossed the shallow river, and began to climb up the stone steps.

Chapter Five

Clueless

As they reached the first level, they saw an opening. With quiet respect, one by one they entered the dwelling. Uri felt as if he were entering into a sanctuary, a hallowed place. A place of the past where people were born, raised families, and died... hundreds, maybe thousands of years ago.

The area was about twenty feet long and fourteen feet wide, but the ceiling was only five feet high, indicating the dwellers must have been small. In the ceiling at the entrance, was an opening to the sky. The "sky light" opening, close to four by eight feet, let in quite a lot of light. These people were quite the engineers. Pieces of slender, decayed wood indicated something long ago latticed across it.

As they stood in the back of the room, the wall in front of them had a large opening for a window, facing the sea. A cool breeze filtered through to the front opening. Against the wall to their right leaned a broken ladder. Many rungs were missing and the wood was very decayed. It led up to an arched opening to the room above.

Uri looked around for a clue or sign that the men they saw were here, but nothing was on the floor, except some stones, bits of broken pottery, and dusty pieces of twigs in the corners. These men, determined to stop those believing in The Creator, were careful not to leave behind any damaging evidence.

In silence, Coran exited, followed by the rest, and climbed the carefully placed stones to the next level. Again, one by one, they entered. This level was smaller by four feet.

An opening, although smaller than the level below, looked out to the sea. In addition, a ladder, knocked askew, pointed to the next level. The third level was the same as the second, and the fourth level was smaller, but you had to find a way to climb into it.

As they made their way to the next dwelling, no one had spoken a word, only looked around, and at each other in amazement. The first thing they noticed when they entered the next dwelling was the darkened wall. Ancient soot revealed an area stained with many years of fires.

"I think this is where a family unit lived." Abosol whispered.

"Yes, that makes sense. Each dwelling has four levels and the bottom level is like a central area, the upper ones private rooms for the families. Twenty people could live here together, comfortably." Denar nodded.

"The top level has no openings. Maybe the children slept there. It would have been the safest place." Coran added. "Were they protecting them from animals or...other people?"

Uri shook his head in wonder. "Good question. But where did they come from and ...where did they go? Why did they go?"

"Maybe they were our ancestors." Denar said.

"Maybe a disease or war killed them off." Uri speculated.

"Maybe we will probably never know." Denar said.

Suddenly, Uri felt strange. The hair on his arms began to stand up. Was someone watching? On the other hand, was it just the creepy thought of the many lives that existed here so long ago? Like ancient, ghostly figures moving from shadow to shadow. The morning light began pouring over the tall dwellings, and entered into the levels. It was even more ominous. Uri went outside and took a deep breath.

"Have you seen enough?" Denar asked everyone.

Uri answered. "I've seen more than enough."

He shuddered. Ghosts? No, only ghostly thoughts. Did anyone know about this place? Were there other haunting dwellings scattered about this land? Uri's curious mind could continue asking questions indefinitely. However, for every question there were no answers…yet.

As they climbed, Abosol called out. "Look here…a pile of burnt wood and coals." On the side of the trail, a large pile of debris scattered about.

Denar took a stick and poked around. "There are old coals below these smoldering ones."

"Those men have been here before, maybe many times." Abosol stated. "Waiting for their friends to arrive at night."

"This means they have been having these meetings for a long time." Denar looked toward the sea.

When they turned to walk up the path, they stopped. Everyone saw it at once. A large rock, tall and wide stood above them. It was a face of a man. Did someone carve it to look like that, or was their imagination fooling them? Denar climbed up to the front of it. He touched the stony surface.

"Well, I don't know what to think. From down there where you stand, it looks like a face. From up here it looks like a bumpy rock."

No one answered, only continued climbing to the top. Each one as they passed touched and rubbed the rock. Uri was dumbfounded.

With slow, deliberate steps, they followed the trail that led to the footbridge. It was creaky and old, but recently fortified with great knowledge and care.

"This is interesting." Denar noted. "It looks as if someone fixed this bridge."

"Is there someone in our village a good builder, a carpenter?" Abosol asked.

"There is someone who lives out in the area by Zekod's place." Denar cocked his head. "I think his name is Capel. He makes all kinds of small tables and chairs from the large, hard plants in the desert. His specialties are milking stools. But I don't know anything about him."

"We don't want to make accusations until we have proof. Very convenient, this meeting place. Caves to hide in, close to the sea, and no living thing to observe them." Coran nodded looking around.

They finished crossing the bridge, and carefully made their way down to the trail.

They took their time, stopping several times to eat and drink the provisions they carried on their backs, and discussed at great length what they had observed.

"We can't continue to trek up here every day." Denar said. "It was just luck we saw them this time."

"There is no such thing as luck." Coran corrected him. "The Creator arranged it this way."

"I wish He had arranged for us to find some proof." Uri said without thinking…again.

"All in His good time. We don't know how this will play out." Coran patted Uri on the back.

As they sat beside the pathway down from the hills, Uri stretched and walked over to the edge of the road that looked down over the meadows below. He hadn't noticed the rolling green land below when they came up earlier. This is where the Rabirs, a nomadic tribe not only occupied the desert, but also kept their flocks in the lush meadows below the hills. Here pools of water, bubbling up from the fast flowing wells, kept everything green.

Uri spotted a group of five Rabir herdsmen with a large flock of kavacs. They moved in the direction away from the hills so Uri was confident no one saw him, but he stayed behind a large bush anyway, and peeked through it. He was curious, never seeing these people before, and watched as the men tapped their animals with long poles, and shouted at them to move along.

This was a perfect place to herd their kavacs and bameas. From the bamea's fur, they wove a fine cloth. It sold well among the rest of the tribes. The Rabir never came to the marketplace. They remained in their own land, never mingling with the other tribes. Someone from the Yoka and Pinola villages went to the Rabirs and brought rolls of the cloth to sell at the marketplace.

"Hey, what are you doing?" Abosol asked, coming up behind Uri.

"Look, see the Rabir herdsmen, and isn't that a beautiful meadow?"

Abosol stuck his ragged hair next to Uri. He grunted and went back to the group. "Come here Uri, and let me look at your wound before we continue."

Uri reluctantly backed away from the edge of the road and sat down while Abosol poked and looked at the wound. He grunted again. Uri shook his head. He was amused with Abosol's manner. It matched his appearance.

"You have a nasty bruise there, but it will heal in a few days."

Coran looked it over and agreed.

"Stop fussing over me." Uri complained.

It took the good part of the day to reach home. By the time the group reached the Pinola village, darkness had set in. The group went to Denar's home where his wife made a delicious, hot meal. Everyone ate heartily and appreciated her effort.

Denar had previously arranged for Pattis to come to his home after the high hour. Even though it was late into the night, he appeared promptly at the appointed time.

Chapter Six

Reflection

As the aged, rugged man entered, he smiled at all the solemn faces. Only Uri's shone with excitement at what they had found.

"Yesterday was an interesting day, my friends." Pattis began in a low voice. "Zekod did not appear at the council meeting. However, Denar, your successor was there."

"Miltas?" Denar asked.

Denar had removed himself from the Council soon after becoming a follower of The Creator. Everyone wanted him to stay to listen for any information, but Denar didn't want to become a spy.

"Yes, and he strongly opposed any investigation into the poisonings. He said they were the warnings of the spirits. A couple men agreed with him, saying the warnings were valid. Everyone else wanted to investigate. The vote was three to three, so Zekod will have the winning vote. Do you have an idea how he will vote?" Pattis looked coyly at each man.

"Of course he will vote with Miltas." Denar smirked.

"Ah, I thought so." Pattis nodded. "Tell me what you found."

"We did not bring back any proof. Only more suspicions." Abosol said. He shook his shaggy head. "The men we saw were too far away to be sure of positive identification."

"Well, what did you see?"

Coran, being the storyteller and orator, began. "When we reached the sea, there was a shallow river running into it from the hills. Across that river were several cliff dwellings four or five levels high; very ancient, but in splendid condition."

Pattis' eyes grew big. "Ahh… how interesting."

"Then men appeared from within one. I don't know Zekod that well, but I believe that he was one of them."

"There were three Pinolas. I also think one was Zekod, and one of them looked like Pishob." Uri interjected.

"But we aren't sure." Coran glared at Uri. "One was a man from the Bast tribe and one a strange Dombara. They conducted some kind of business. It seemed the Bast gave something to one of the Pinolas. Then the Bast and Dombara went to the sea, got in a boat and began to sail back across the Green Sea. The Pinolas went down to the trail that goes back to the village."

"Did any of them see you?" Pattis asked.

"No, I am sure of that." Coran answered.

Pattis sat forward in his seat. "Tell me about the dwellings. There is an ancient myth about people living in our land before we came here."

"The caves up stretched up high, four and five levels." Uri's eyes grew big with excitement. "The dwellings gave us a strange feeling, as if we had stepped back in time. They have been unoccupied for a very long time. For some reason the people who built them disappeared long ago."

"It looked like a large family could live together in one dwelling, with bedrooms on the upper levels. They are very ancient." Denar said. "We looked through a couple, hoping for any kind of clue the men may have left behind."

Coran finished, "We are disappointed we couldn't bring any back proof of identity of the Pinolas, and what they were receiving."

Uri looked at the floor. "We need a miracle."

"If you followed them and confronted Zekod, what do you think would happen?" Pattis asked.

"Zekod is a desperate man, and believes he is very clever. There is no telling what he would do." Denar answered. "Remember, he is a murderer."

A heavy silence followed.

"Come on, boys," Pattis chided as he sat back in the armchair. He tapped his fingers restlessly. "You must know we can't let these crimes go on. Somehow, they must be solved. If the leaders of the tribe won't do it, you must"

"Can we sneak into Zekod's home when he's away and see what we can find?" Uri asked.

"He has a wife and daughter who never leave the place." Pattis said, "Miltas is unmarried and lives alone, however I could never approve of such a thing." He clucked and shook his head.

"Did Zekod let anyone know he would not be attending the council meeting today?" Coran asked.

"No." Pattis answered. "It is very unusual for any of the members to be absent. We meet only once a week." Pattis stood up; silently announcing the meeting was over.

"After a few days I think members of the council will go out to Zekod's farm, and ask him why he was absent from the meeting without any excuse."

"If you question Zekod, carefully watch his reaction." Denar suggested.

"Well, if you boys come up with any ideas, let me know." Walking slowly, with a limp, Pattis went to the door and walked out, disappearing into the night.

***

Uri dragged himself along the pathway to home and bed. Exhaustion filtered into every fiber of his body. It had been many hours since anyone slept, and the meeting with Pattis seemed to drag on. While they walked along in the dark, Uri turned to Coran. "Today, when we spotted the men, there was a Dombara with the Bast. Do you have any idea why?"

"No. I didn't recognize him. He was a Dombara, but not dressed as one."

"His hair was cropped short, like the Bast wear theirs." Uri paused, thinking before he spoke again. "It's strange. There is something familiar about the way he moved. It reminded me of someone, but I can't place who it could be."

"They were too far for me to clearly see or make out any features. I couldn't hear much of what they were saying either." Coran noted.

"Zekod and his gang have been very careful. He is a clever one." Uri said.

"I am going to go home in a couple days." Coran opened the door of Uri's home and waited for him to go inside first.

Uri shut the door behind him, and bolted it. "I hope we get this solved soon. I would like to go back to Dombara Land with you. I miss everyone, especially Bibbi, Jai, and Luwanna. I get lonely here, away from friends my age."

"Is school over for the year?" Coran asked.

"Yes, it will be four weeks before it starts again. With the Festival of the Full Moons next week, I would like to go with you and spend some time with my friends. Beka is busy with her marketplace and Suwat is hardly home anymore. Between helping to build Ovi pens, and instructing the men on how to make nets for fishing, he has really found his niche." They went directly to the bedroom.

"I think it would be a good idea to come back with me to Dombara Land. We can only do so much here anyway. In the end, it is up to the officials of the village to solve any crime. The Festival of the Full Moons will be a grand affair. After the 'viewing', everyone will be at the Great Hall and there will be quite a feast. Jinela will be playing her instrument, and there will be singing. You can visit and stay until school begins. I will gladly take you home."

Uri became excited. "That sounds wonderful. I can't wait."

"We must remember the people in this land. The unbelievers will be making sacrifices to the Evil Spirits on that night. Our people must be very aware and extremely careful." Coran warned.

"The Followers are planning to be together. There is safety in numbers, so they will spend the night camped in the caves by the Green Sea. No one will bother them there. The unbelievers can raise all the ruckus they want." Uri said grimly. "Our people will be far away from it." He fell silent then turned and faced Coran. "Are you going to tell me how you obtained the poison?"

Coran grinned. "It bothers you that everything you want to know isn't immediately available."

"Yes. I suppose it does." Uri lay back on his sleeping mat, irritated.

"When the time is right, you will know." Coran yawned.

Chapter Seven
Quiet Interlude

The next day was uneventful. Uri and Coran went to the marketplace and walked around looking for someone or something that seemed out of place. Denar held the Believer meetings at his home in the evening. Once a week everyone came together to pray, hear passages from the Holy Book and a message, given by one of the elders of the group. Only a few believers considered mature enough in the faith, were elevated to the position of elder. Koori, who was their priest, Denar, and a new addition from Dombara land, a young man named Gradis. As soon as he arrived, a young Pinola woman began to follow him around and he seemed to enjoy the attention from her.

Their talks lasted about twenty minutes and focused on how to live life according to The Creator's design. How to behave toward each other and how to show the Way by being kind and giving, something the Pinolas had never practiced before.

Uri volunteered to set up for the meetings, and along with Reena, the job went smoothly, among jokes and good-natured banter. Today after searching the market place, Uri and Coran walked over to Denar's hut to join Reena, and between the three of them, it took no time to finish the job. Tonight Coran planned to speak to the people. Everyone enjoyed the few times Coran could be with them, so Uri knew it would be crowded.

At the beginning of the evening, the Believers began to arrive. The little home filled to overflowing, and some late comers stood listening and watching from the window openings and the doorway. They prayed among themselves and prayed for each other.

Then the leader read passages from one of the Holy Books. Coran stood at the best vantage point in the front room. He bowed to the congregation of people, and took a deep breath.

"We know most of you have been affected in some way with persecution from the few agitators among the tribe. The woman, Letura, found a few days ago in the desert, consumed a poison. She died. Two others are recovering from the same type of poisoning."

The people muttered among themselves. Most everyone knew about Letura's fate.

"We don't have any idea how the three victims received the poison, so be very careful. Be suspicious of everyone, especially at the marketplace. However, we do have an idea how the poison got here, and who is involved. Keep a sharp eye out and report anything suspicious to Pattis or Denar."

"Who do you think is guilty?" The question came from the back of the room.

"It doesn't matter who we suspect. Watch everyone you come in contact with."

Coran bowed his head. "We need our Lord to intervene and send us evidence."

"Will that happen? Is our Lord that involved in our lives?" A woman, a friend of Letura, asked with tears in her eyes.

43

"Does He move in such a personal way?" Another asked from outside the window opening.

"Yes." Coran replied emphatically. "The Holy Books remind us that our Lord cares and loves us, and He watches over each and every one of us. We are His children, and He delivers us from the snares of those who try to harm us. The Creator pours His love into our hearts. He loves and protects His own."

"He didn't protect Letura." A grumble came from outside the window.

Coran straightened and raised his voice. "Shall we insist The Creator tell us all His plans? Trusting Him is what faith is. She is gone. She has become a martyr for the faith. Our Lord used her for His purposes, not ours. The Lord shall sustain us in our sorrow. However, if we continually question Him and fall away... our faith will run cold, and we will find ourselves back in unbelief and empty again. He loves us and wants the best for us. So trust in the Lord. He will make you strong and joyful."

Koori stood, holding three-month-old Ranui. "Brothers and sisters, we are like a herd of kavacs." He referred to the small, furry, hoofed animals almost everyone owned. We wander around in our pens, not knowing whether to go this way or that. Our Lord comes and leads us. He guides and steers us on the path in life. Because of Him, we have no needs. He restores our spirit. Even if we walk in danger, and death is around us, He is there to comfort us. He provides us with more than we could ever hope for. Therefore, if we continue to read his Word, trust in Him, and follow Him all our lives, we will dwell with Him forever."

This brought tears to many eyes and the people cried, "Yes, so be it."

As the commotion died down, Coran raised his arms and called out the blessing on the people. "Go and pray...each one of you. We will see the movement of our Lord among us."

Uri listened and nodded. He knew of the personal protection of The Creator. He personally received a miracle on the sand bar as he lay dying of thirst. He asked The Creator into his heart and suddenly, Coran, who had received a vision, arrived in a boat. He prayed Coran would receive another vision, as he did that day; a vision showing how to prove their suspicions of Zekod, and his gang.

Chapter Eight

Aleeta

She stood at the edge of the village shivering. Not because she was cold, but because she was afraid. In all her twenty-three years, Aleeta had never left her farm. However, tonight she watched the moons overhead send their friendly light to guide her way, but the task in front of her was daunting. If her father awoke, and discovered her gone, he most surely would find her and kill her.

Clutching the tiny pouch, she looked behind her, trembling. Nothing was on the horizon. No one followed her. All she had to do was continue into the village and find the man named Denar.

She had come in the middle of the night. That was the only time she could get away. However, no one was stirring in the village "Go!" she whispered to herself. "Just go and maybe someone will see you and help."

Barefoot, step by step, she walked along the path into the area of surrounding huts. She continued down the path, looking to see if any of the side trails had a sign, or name by the huts.

Aleeta was proud she could read. Not because of anything her parents did. She learned to read from her brother Jai, or used-to-be brother. She missed him terribly. He was the only one of her family who was kind to her.

She slowly made her way to the market place and looking around cautiously, she pressed the pouch to her chest. *"This has to be done."* She thought. Many times in the recent past, she had listened from the bedroom as the men planned terrible things.

They always shut the women up in the tiny bedroom, while their men schemed and strategized. Her mother and the two other women brought by their husbands, pretended not to know what was going on, but Aleeta laid on the cold floor near the door, listening. This time she discovered the object of the attack were the leaders of the new religion. The poison, just obtained, was different and the results were horrible. Late that night, in the darkness, she crept to the front room and grabbed the pouch that contained the vial. Without a sound, she left the house, and ran down the road, frantic. Had she been discovered? Was someone following her? Now she was here in the village, alone. However, soon her father would discover the missing vial, along with his missing daughter.

She leaned against one of the stalls, slid down, and sat crouched on the ground. Aleeta covered her feet with the tattered dress, and looked at her red, sore hands. Most of the time, her hands were dirty and stained from slopping around in the animal pens, a job she inherited when Jai disappeared. Weeks would go by, then, without warning, her mother would arise from a tearful, melancholy state and wake Aleeta early in the morning. A bucket of dirty water and a bar of a nasty brown soap thrust into her hands and together, they spent hours of scrubbing and scraping at the filth in the house. Her mother made those bars of soap from something harsh and caustic.

Soon Aleeta's hands were raw and sore. Her knees chafed with open sores. In a few days, her mother was back into her melancholy state again. Nothing stayed clean for long. Her father and brothers stomped through the house with filth-covered boots. Dirty and coarse, they spit on the floors she just scrubbed without a thought to the rough bar of soap she used a few hours ago. Something was wrong with this kind of a life. Instinct told her this was not the way to live.

She yawned and tried to get comfortable. She hadn't eaten or had any water for a couple of days. Her stomach cramped with hunger pain. Maybe someone would come to the marketplace early. She would watch from her hiding place in case someone came along. Then she would act as if she just arrived, and ask about Denar. Even though she tried not to sleep, she briefly nodded off.

"Hey you there, girl. Who are you and what do you want here?"

The voice startled Aleeta and she jumped to her feet, feeling for the small pouch in her hands.

"Please sir, I am looking for a man named Denar and his wife Reena. Could you tell me, which path I take to their home?"

"Well, you go straight down to the left and turn at the first path to the right. You'll find it. It's the only one without a talisman in front." The man leaned over, raising his bushy eyebrows. "What do you want with them?"

"I'm a friend and I haven't seen them for a while." She lied. "Just want to visit." She put on a weak smile.

"They'll be awake by now. Off with you."

She thanked him and left as fast as her sore feet would take her. Staggering down the streets, dizziness followed her. The sun was just beginning to rise as she found the hut without a talisman. She knocked on the front door, and when it opened, she almost fell inside. "Are you Denar and is your wife Reena?"

A sleepy-eyed man stepped back with surprise. "Yes."

"I have something for you. Something you have been looking for." She handed him the pouch. "It contains a poison." Her eyes rolled up and she fell to the floor unconscious.

The next thing Aleeta saw was Reena's soft brown eyes looking into hers." No, don't try to get up." Reena said. "You were so cold that we wrapped you up in a blanket, and laid you on our bed. Denar is getting you something warm to drink."

"Thank you." She answered in a weak voice.

Denar came in the bedroom with a steaming cup of crost. "Are you feeling better?"

"Yes." She took the cup in her hands.

"Can you tell us who you are?" Denar began.

"My name is Aleeta. Zekod is my father."

Reena gasped and looked to Denar.

"I brought you the poison he came home with the night before last. The men lock us up in a room when they make their plans. I've listened and heard about the people they have poisoned. Now this is something much worse, and they plan to use it on you and some others... I don't know what to do. I can't stand it anymore." She broke into tears.

Reena put her arm around Aleeta, and hugged her tight. "That's all right. You cry all you want. You are safe with us."

"He is s-s-so cruel." Aleeta sobbed. "If he finds out I stole it, he'll kill me."

"You are with us now. He won't be able to touch you." Denar said firmly. "Tell us what you heard."

Aleeta took a deep breath. "It is my father and my brothers who are using the poison. Miltas and another man are in on it too. Someone contacted them from across the sea a couple of months ago. I never heard any names. They promised them a way to defeat your new beliefs."

"Do you know what they wanted in return?"

"Yes, me for one… and other women."

Reena gasped again. "For what purpose?"

Aleeta whispered, "Slavery." her eyes wide with terror.

"I must get Coran and Uri right away." Denar rushed to grab his staff. No one went anywhere anymore without a staff to defend themselves.

Aleeta stood up, fear rippling across her back.

Denar reached back to touch her arm. "No, don't be afraid. They are my friends and Believers." He looked at Reena. "I'll be right back. Get her something to eat."

"Are you hungry?" Reena smiled.

"Yes. The men were so excited over this new thing," referring to the poison, "they forgot to let the women eat for the last couple of days."

Reena sighed. "Well let's get something right now." She motioned for Aleeta to follow her into the kitchen. Soon the wonderful smell of fresh biscuits and meat filled the hut. Aleeta tried not to gobble the food, but it was so good and she was so hungry, her plate was empty in an instant.

"Are you still hungry?" Reena asked.

Aleeta, her mouth full, nodded.

"I'll tell you what. When the men get back, I'll go out to the ovi coop and bring in a bunch of eggs and scramble them all up."

"Oh no!" Aleeta was alarmed. "I heard they are very bad and make people sick."

"That's a lie. Eggs are very good for you, very healthy. You must trust us. We eat eggs all the time. The birds, the ovis are cute little things. Your father lied to you. See how lies frighten people?" Reena asked, and poured crost in her cup.

As Aleeta finished her breakfast, Denar was back with Uri and Coran. When Coran walked in the door, his robe flying around him, Aleeta felt an electric shock. He was so handsome, his golden hair loose around his face while the rest fell braided down his back. When he smiled at her with his kind eyes, she felt safe in a strange and comforting way.

"Well hello." He greeted her, and his voice made her heart melt inside her body

She just looked at him, not saying a word. He wrapped his robes around him and knelt beside her. "So you are Zekod's daughter. Thank you for being so brave, and bringing us the evidence we need to stop the poisonings."

She didn't hear a word he said. Her eyes followed him as he accepted a cup of crost, and pulled a pillow over to sit on next to her. She looked at the long slender hand and fingers protruding from the open sleeves in the robe. "Are you a god?" She asked

Everyone laughed and she felt her face turn red.

"No Aleeta. I am a Dombara priest. Are you an angel?"

"No- I don't think so." She didn't know what an angel was.

They smiled at each other a long time.

"Well, I think it is time we find out what this is all about." Denar butted in.

"Oh, right." Coran stood up over Aleeta. "We need to ask you some questions, so let us go into the front room where you will be comfortable." He extended his hand and when she took it, Aleeta wished he would never let go.

Chapter Nine
Convicting Evidence

Coran listened to Aleeta tell about the things she had overheard. When she finished, he asked her if she could read and write.

"Yes, I can." She replied proudly. Coran gave her an instrument they used to make marks on the coarse paper bark, stripped from the Paper Tree.

"Write down everything you told me," he instructed her.

It was early in the afternoon by the time Aleeta finished writing down her testimony that she would read to the council.

Before dinner, Denar and Uri went to Pattis and told him about Aleeta's testimony. Pattis immediately sent messengers calling for an emergency meeting, late the next afternoon.

By then, the news of about Zekod's daughter coming to town, and the damaging evidence she had, spread though the village. The Meeting Hall quickly filled to capacity, which forced many villagers to gather at the doors. However, Miltas and Zekod were missing. The messenger reported they were not in their homes.

Aleeta stood before the five attending council members. She looked briefly at the men, expecting her father to come roaring in at any moment. Her hands were visibly shaking. She wore a print dress Reena loaned her. It was a soft green with tiny white flowers scattered about, and it tied at the waist. The pair of sandals Uri found for her felt tight and uncomfortable, however she knew she must adjust to new things. Beka had fixed her hair, twisting it around her head. She felt pretty for the first time in her life.

"Th-thank you gentlemen. I have a statement to read." She paused, straightened her shoulders, and took a deep breath." I am Aleeta, daughter of Zekod and Ambora. Many nights in the past months, my father and brothers, Pishob and Turik, have met with other men; by name...Miltas, Fewbin. Also, Capel, the village carpenter. They locked all the women in an adjoining room. The wives sat huddled together, but I lay on the floor, night after night by the door, and pretended to be asleep. I listened and heard many terrible plans, but the last was the worst, and I knew I had to stop them from carrying it out.

"They contacted men from the Bast tribe through a Dombara they knew. I don't know his name. They called him 'The Dombara'. They obtained a poison, and my father chose people of our Pinola tribe, new to The Way, that would be their victims. I understand the last one died. A few days ago, they brought home a vial that contained a different poison. It would do terrible things to people, so I decided to steal it and bring it here. I did this at the risk of my life. My father will most certainly kill me. I gave the vial to Denar... Now I need sanctuary. I hope I have done the right thing. Thank you for listening to me." She visibly shuddered as she finished her speech.

"When did these meetings begin?" The eldest member of the council asked.

"Soon after the boy, Uri came home. My father, brothers, and several men met many times, trying to think of ways to discourage people from listening to Uri. When The Way

54

appeared to be catching on, and people were turning against the Spirits, they grew more desperate and thought of others things. Things like spreading lies and fear among the villagers. For instance, telling everyone the damaging winds last year were brought on by the Spirits."

"When did they start talking about the poisons?" Pattis asked.

"About three months ago." Aleeta continued, feeling braver all the time. "They seemed to know they could get something from across the sea. That is when they began to talk about The Dombara. Some of the men stopped coming to the meetings, but those I mentioned stayed and were anxious to continue. The Dombara even came to our hut once. I could hear them talking through the locked door. He mentioned he could obtain what they were looking for from the Bast people."

Pattis stood up and bowed in respect to Aleeta. "My child, you certainly have done the right thing. Now Denar, will you continue the story?"

"Yes. To the most honored council. When Aleeta brought me the vial I immediately called on Coran, our Dombara priest, and had him examine it. He confirmed it was a poison used by the Bast tribe that brought coma and after many days, death. It is an extremely potent poison, and always results in death. The Bast do not know of an antidote. However, there is a rumor that there is one, although only a very few people know of it."

"Do you have this vial with you?" Pattis asked.

"Yes." Denar handed the vial to Pattis who placed it in front of him on the table. The five men seated at the council table strained to look at it. No one wanted to touch it, however.

"How do we know you are telling the truth?" One of them asked.

"Give it to an animal, and if it falls into a coma and dies after many weeks, you will know I tell the truth", Coran spoke up. "Please be advised, before it falls into a coma it will suffer, greatly."

"I don't think we need to do that." Pattis said. "The fact that Zekod and Miltas are absent confirms your story. However, why would the Bast Tribe give Zekod something for nothing? Was there something they wanted in return? If not, this story makes no sense. "

"Oh yes," Coran added, "there was something they asked for. Tell them Aleeta."

She stood, her eyes filled with tears. "The Dombara asked for women."

"Women?" Pattis narrowed his eyes. "What do you mean?"

"My father promised to give the Dombara… me for one, and other women in the tribe, young women, to sell for… for slaves."

A gasp arose from throughout the people assembled. The question audibly circulated, "What are slaves?"

Denar turned to face the people. "This word is not often used among us, but some understand. Slavery is to take people against their will and keep them for any purpose the slave owner desires. A slave has no rights, no dignity, and no power of resistance." Denar added. "It is an abomination."

"Why would the Bast want slaves?" The doubting council member asked.

Denar put up his hands to quiet everyone. "Tell them." He motioned to Aleeta.

"The Bast didn't want to keep us," Aleeta squeezed back the tears. "The Dombara said the Bast were going to sell us to another tribe; a secret tribe."

This surprised even Uri and Coran.

As the gathering began to calm down, Pattis stood and lifted his hands over the assembled people "This is unprecedented in our history. We have no guidelines to go by, so we will have to vote on how to handle this situation."

"I suggest we go to Zekod and ask him to tell us his side." the old council member offered. They all agreed.

"Let us dismiss and convene in an hour at Zekod's home." Pattis ruled.

Aleeta weakly leaned against Reena and Denar. "Oh please, don't let them make me go too."

"Don't worry." Coran leaned over her. "You go back to Denar's home and rest. It will be all right."

Reena took Aleeta home, had her lay down on a mat in the back bedroom. She covered the window so the light wouldn't shine in and Aleeta could rest.

Aleeta laid thinking for a long time. She remembered things she wished she had added to her testimony. She remembered the first time she heard her father tell her mother the Evil Spirits that ruled this land had blessed him. Because they had touched him, he had a mark on his face that all could see. People knew this mark meant he could contact the Spirits and give people advice. He could tell them what to do that would remove a curse from them or their animals. It didn't matter if it was true or not, Zekod's mark was visible proof he had power.

He could control people by telling them they must take his advice, and give him many gifts. Whatever he asked for, he got, whether it be food, animals, or valuables. His attitude was one of arrogance and he distrusted anyone who did not bow to him.

Aleeta realized she never knew how dangerous and evil her father was, until now.

Chapter Ten

Banishment

Uri and Coran, followed by many townspeople, walked behind the rest of the council to Zekod's farm. Denar and Abosol lead the way.

The stench coming from the animals and their pens filled their nostrils, added to the atmosphere of depravity that oppressed the very air they breathed. Many covered their noses. Pishob and Turik met the group at the front of the hut.

With a menacing frown, Pishob stared, glowering eyes looking from face to face. "What do you want?"

Uri looked at them one at a time. Pishob put on his father's angry face, but Turik looked frightened.

"Where is your father?" asked Pattis.

"He's gone away for a few days."

"There are serious charges against you, your brother, and your father. We are going to take you back to the council hall and ask you some questions."

"Nobody's taking us anywhere."

Coran, Denar and Abosol, along with two other men from the council stepped forward, exposing long spears.

"Yes we are." Abosol stated flatly.

59

Turik doubled up clutching his stomach. "I knew it. I knew we'd get in trouble."

"Shut up, you whining coward." his brother yelled.

"You're the one, Pishob. I didn't want nothin' to do with it. Pappy said we had to participate." He was almost in tears.

"Where are Miltas, Fewbin, and Capel?" Denar asked as he pushed the two brothers ahead of him.

"They went with our Pappy." Turik said.

"And where is your mother?" Pattis broke in. "You realize the wife of a criminal is as guilty as he is."

"Leave her alone. She didn't do nothin." Turik pleaded.

"Unfortunately we can't do that. The law is the law." Pattis motioned for Abosol to go to the door of the hut.

As he opened it, they all were appalled at the scene inside. It was as if the animals lived in the house as well as out. Ambora stood in the middle of the mess, tears leaving tracks in the dirt on her face.

"Please don't hurt me." she whispered.

"We won't hurt you. Come with us." Abosol spoke gently.

Slowly she walked out, and stood with her sons. She wiped her face with the tattered apron around her tiny waist, and stood as tall as she could.

"My boys are good boys. They didn't do nothin' wrong."

"According to your daughter, you have."

"Aleeta is a liar!" She hissed from between her teeth.

"She gave us the vial, stolen from your husband." Pattis said. "You will come with us now." He called two of the council

60

members over to him. "Go to the homes of the others, and see if they are really gone. Bring their wives back with you."

***

The council members found the homes of Miltas and Fewbin next to each other. Their wives looked old and sickly. When told of the circumstances one began to sob while the other remained stoic, stumbling along without a word. Finding Capel's home, however, was more difficult.

"Who can tell us where Capel lives?" Ketri, one of the council members asked.

Neither woman would cooperate.

"Fine," he said. "Then we will go house to house until we locate him."

Dragging the women along the group finally found someone knew who Capel was and where he lived.

When the two men, their prisoners in tow, reached the designated home they called Capel's name, but no one answered.

"What do you think we should do?" Ketri asked the older man.

"I think we should open the door and see if he is hiding inside."

The door was locked. So, together the two men broke down the door and entered the darkened, rundown hut. In front of them was the body of Capel, his throat slit from ear to ear and blood everywhere.

"Oh no!" Ketri gasped. Neither of the men had ever heard of a tribe member taking his own life. They stared horrified, then rushed out the door, closing it behind them, and swiftly headed for the center of the village.

By the time the men arrived back in the village with Zekod's family and the other wives, word had spread to everyone. This was the biggest gathering anyone could remember. Crowds gathered at the Council Hall, trading gossip and rumors.

As the group approached, awkward silence blanketed the crowd. The men cleared a way for them all to walk into the hall. Pishob kept his head down and tried to cover his face, while Turik looked from person to person, whimpering. Ambora flashed angry eyes at those staring at her. As soon as they all disappeared behind the walls, chatter began among the crowd again.

The sun had set and evening was upon the land. It was dark in the Council Hall. A woman came and lit all the lamps in the room, but there remained an eerie twilight. Finally, a torch was brought in from outside and the shadows disappeared from the walls.

Immediately the facts and charges were presented and each suspect had a chance to speak his or her piece to defend themselves. Pishob remained defiant, while Turik remained pathetic. The women begged for mercy. However, at the end, every one of the council members agreed. Zekod, Pishob and Turik, Miltas, and Fewbin, were guilty of murder and other crimes.

Ambora, along with two other wives stood apart from the men. Everyone in the village remained outside straining to see and hear what was taking place. Inside, Aleeta stood with Reena, Beka, Uri, and Coran.

Uri watched Aleeta's face. What was she thinking, and would she be able to contain her emotions?

Pattis stood at the head of the council. Uri could see his face was grey, and saddened by the day's events. His aging features reflected in the flickering lights.

"This is a sad day in our history. Having no place for imprisonment, we need to find a punishment."

He stopped and took a deep breath. "We, elders of the Pinola Tribe, banish you all from Pinola Land. We will confiscate your land, animals, and belongings, selling them to the highest bidders. This punishment is to take place immediately. We will provide each one of you with warm clothing, and a ration of water and bread. You will be taken to the edge of the town limits, into the desert, and forbidden to return for the rest of your lives, under threat of death."

The noise in the Council Hall tumbled out into the crowds outside. Pandemonium rolled over the people, standing in the dark. This was an unprecedented event, and everyone seemed to be voicing his or her own opinion all at once.

Uri could see the trauma Aleeta displayed in her face. Seeing her family banished punished her as well. He would rather see all of them imprisoned, so the Believers would be able to talk to them about The Creator. Uri believed they eventually would understand. However, the council members were not Believers, so they did what they thought was right in their eyes.

Aleeta wept as her mother and brothers, hands bound, were ushered out the door by several men.

Ambora looked back. "You!" she screamed at her daughter. "You caused this. May the Spirits curse you and eat away your insides, till you fall dead!"

Everyone within earshot gasped. It was appalling to hear a mother say that to her daughter." *What kind of people were* they?" Uri thought, *"The Evil One must have them under his influence in a mighty way."*

Aleeta fell to the floor. Great sobs escaped from deep within her. Coran rushed to her, picked her up, and held her to his chest. "Hush, hush" he repeated in her ear.

Uri knew all this damaged her emotionally, and she would need time to recover. How could they help her? How could they help to heal her soul? He prayed the Savior would grant her strength, and Coran would use his wisdom to guide her back to health.

Chapter Eleven
Transitions

It was the next day. Coran, Denar, and Reena sat in Uri's home with Beka and Suwat. Beka held Aleeta in her arms as she curled up in a tight ball.

Uri sat on the floor, hugging his knees to his chest. "I think it was wrong to banish them. If they were here we could teach them the Way."

Coran sighed and looked into the distance. "You must accept the fact that some people will never come to know the Savior."

Uri didn't believe it. He thought the council took the easy way to get rid of the problem. "Do you mean to say, there are some The Creator can't reach?" Uri knew better, but was baiting his cousin.

"No, that's not what I'm saying. We all have free choice in that matter. However, there are people who are so deep into rebellion they refuse salvation. The Creator leaves them to their own devices."

"If we put them in a hut and detain them there for a year or so, we could tell them about The Creator over and over. Don't you think they would eventually understand and believe? I think that is what should have been done." Uri pouted. He grumbled because no one thought he had good ideas.

"So, you are saying, to make people understand who The Creator is, we need to lock everyone up, and hammer the truth into them? Coran asked.

"Well, when you put it that way, no." Uri turned his head and pursed his lips together. He didn't like the way his words were twisted.

"When the Savior was walking among the people, He told them and offered them the Truth. The Truth will set us free, but we must accept it of our own free will." Coran tried to explain. "Perhaps some people need to be told the story over and over again, in different ways, but when it is refused, forcing our belief on people does not work."

"Well, now we will never get the chance to tell it to them, over and over again, will we?" Uri was sullen.

Coran looked long and hard at Uri. "We don't bring people to The Creator. We tell them, and He does the work. We are only His messengers. Once they have been told, we allow The Spirit to do His part."

"In other words, I am trying to do The Creator's part in this?"

"Yes, He didn't choose you to pound The Way into their heads. You offer it, and you plant the seed. Then it is up to them to decide. You allow The Creator's Spirit to work in them."

"If they choose themselves over The Creator, He eventually gives them up to their depravities. Is that right?" Denar asked.

"Right, remember, many are called, few are chosen. Uri, you are one of the few. The Lord has a great mission for you. Don't waste your time on those who will trample your words of righteousness into the mud."

Uri understood what Coran was saying, but that was not how he felt. Everyone was worthy of his time and effort to teach The Way, and share the Good News of the Savior.

Aleeta stirred and opened her eyes. She asked Coran, "Do you think my mother will die in the desert?"

"They will find a nomad tribe and join them." Coran told Aleeta, trying to comfort her, but she showed no reaction.

Uri nodded to Coran and Denar to follow him into the kitchen. As they entered, Coran put one finger to his lips.

"So…" Uri whispered, "Where did Zekod and the others escape to?"

"It has to be the Bast Tribe." Denar nodded.

"I believe you are right." Coran agreed. "We need to do two things. I will enlist some people from my tribe to see if Zekod has gone to the Bast village. Denar get Abosol, and gather people from the Pinolas. Look in all abandoned dwellings and caves to see if he is hiding in one of them.

"I'll go with you to Dombara Land." volunteered Uri. Realizing his surly outlook was unkind, he wanted to show them he repented. "I'm sorry about my attitude. I want to do anything I can for the Good News."

Coran put his arm around Uri and gave him a hug. "When we get to Dombara Land, we can carefully select a group to travel through the forest, quietly and undercover."

Denar frowned. "I'm afraid Aleeta will be slow to heal from the nightmare of seeing her mother and two brothers arrested and banished."

Coran voiced his concern. "Even though she lived under their brutality, the destruction of her family has torn into her soul." Quickly he turned to Uri. "I know, we can bring her with us to visit Jai, her brother."

"That's an excellent idea." Uri beamed. Everyone knew Jai wasn't her real brother. He was one of the Dombara children kidnapped and taken back by his real tribe, just as Uri was. However, Aleeta still talked of Jai as her brother, and retained an emotional connection to him. "We can go after Zekod, and help Aleeta at the same time."

Back in the main room of the home, Aleeta was sitting up and talking. "I miss my mother and worry about her safety."

"Of course, and you will for some time. This is natural, but remember she has your brothers to help her along." Beka replied as she stroked Aleeta's cinnamon colored hair.

Coran rushed into the room, a look of anticipation on his face. "Aleeta, would you like to visit Jai?"

"Oh, yes. Can I ... can we…?"

"Sure, we will go tomorrow in fact."

Aleeta began to cry tears of joy.

Coran held her hands in his. "You know, things will be all right."

Aleeta blinked through her tears and nodded.

Uri believed with love and care, and this opportunity, she would slowly begin to come out of her shell, and realize people were kind and good. Not like her family and her father's friends. Jai would be good for her.

Already she no longer acted as the frightened, ragged woman-child that staggered into their lives with the incriminating evidence. That took extraordinary courage. Uri saw the workings of The Spirit, and knew she could become a great warrior for The Creator. Aleeta needed to get away from

68

the bad memories, and Uri knew she looked forward to seeing Jai again. Most of all, Uri knew she wanted to be with Coran. Everyone could see she was infatuated with him. His presence, with the robes and his authority, captivated her, but he hadn't caught on.

Uri was looking forward to seeing his family, and friends. However, most of all, Uri looked forward to helping Coran find Zekod and the other men. This would provide him with the opportunity of explaining how wonderful knowing The Creator of All could be.

***

Aleeta looked out the back room window into the darkening sky, not yet illuminated by the moons. This is where she stayed since she came to Denar and Reena's home. They offered her comfort and affection. It was the first time she had a room of her very own. All the things she had acquired since her arrival lay on the table in the corner. A dress, a pair of sandals, a beaded necklace, and a beautiful bracelet made from shells Coran gave her yesterday. She danced around the room in a thin gown for sleeping that Beka made especially for her.

Why were these people so kind? They didn't know anything about her a few days ago. Yet everyone treated her with love and kindness. So much had happened in that time. Being a prisoner in her home, she was not able to understand it all. Her father wielded absolute power over everyone, and treated her as property. His temper became the ruling guide to his life. The boys also behaved like Zekod. Cruelty was their best friend. Both got their own way by using fiendish sadism. Pishob and Turik's main object of their savagery was Jai.

Her father did not want another child, and when her mother, Ambora came home with Jai, he was furious. However, the new baby Jai was the delight of Aleeta's life. She

69

was the one who raised him. Ambora let her take over. Still, as soon as the child was able, Zekod sent him to work in the animal pens.

When he disappeared with the rest of the children, her mother sobbed for days. She bemoaned the fact she let him stay in the village with his friend Rill that night. Aleeta wept also, but quiet and alone, because Zekod finally had heard enough, and every time Ambora mentioned Jai, he hit her. It did not take long before no one mentioned his name again.

After Jai left, her brothers seemed to leave her alone; instead they swaggered out into the village, finding the weak, and small to pick on. They got their final justice, but not her mother. She was a victim as surely as Aleeta was.

About to give way to the familiar sadness, she said to herself. *"No."* This must be put behind her. Looking into the crude mirror Aleeta saw her reflection. Gone were the dark circles under her eyes, and the bruises that always marred her body in one place or another. She thought of Coran, and her face tingled to her ears. She would be leaving with him and Uri in the morning, happy to be with him, no matter where he went.

A new life was beginning; a life of freedom and hopefully, maybe…love.

Chapter Twelve
Across the Sea

Uri woke to a day dawning brightly. The clear blue sky promised a good voyage, as today the three of them would leave for Dombara Land. Coran needed to get back to his duties at the temple, and Aleeta needed to get away from painful reminders.

A group of Believers had followed the long way down to the water's edge to say good-bye. Not only to Coran, but goodbye to Uri and Aleeta too. Uri would be gone until school started, and Aleeta voiced that she had no idea when, or if she would ever come back to the home village. There was nothing left for her here.

After tearful and happy wishes for a safe trip, Denar and Abosol pushed the boat out into the water and as the wind caught the sail, the group waved until Uri could no longer see them.

Besides visiting with his friends, why was he going along? He told Coran he wanted to be among those looking for Zekod, yet he knew this was extremely dangerous. He didn't have to go. There were many others, trained in using weapons, and knowledgeable in the ways of the Bast. There was an empty, hollow feeling, growing in the pit of his stomach. He knew in the depths of his being that he was going through a door, one that would shut behind him, leaving no escape.

Although the sky was a cloudless deep blue, wind created white caps, and the sea was choppy. Aleeta sat at the bow and grasped the seat tightly with her fingers.

Coran looked from Aleeta to Uri. "Don't worry. I have sailed in waters like this many times. We will be fine. In fact, this wind will help us to get to Dombara Land faster. This is not a storm, is it Uri?"

"Uh… no, not really." Uri recalled the violence of the sea when he and Rill stole Coran's boat and tried to cross in a real storm. That was when, in anger, Rill tipped the boat over and was lost at sea. Uri hung onto the large paddle and woke up on a desolate sand bar. He would have died if Coran hadn't found him. Then Uri smiled remembering that was when he accepted the Lord of the Universe. "Our Creator will take care of us, Aleeta." He said.

"I don't know who The Creator is. I only know of the Evil Spirits we have in our land and how they took over my family."

Coran spoke up. "Those are lies. Lies to frighten and control the people. The One who created this universe and everything you see is loving and good. He interacts with us, and in order to save us from eternal death, He sent His son into the Universe to die for our sins. So you see, Evil Spirits have no power over you, if you believe."

"I'm confused."

"Do you believe something caused all this to exist?"

"Yes, I guess so. It had to come from something, and evil spirits couldn't create such a beautiful place, all the stars and flowers. The sea and land, it's all so magnificent."

"This is created out of love. You can find the love in everything around us."

"But what about the bad things, like what my father did?"

"There is evil, and people are tempted by greed and lust to choose the evil side."

Aleeta looked up at the sky and sighed, deeply.

"You will understand more as time goes on." Coran promised.

Uri cocked his head as he looked at Aleeta. "Rill was Jai's friend, wasn't he?"

"Yes, he was good to Jai, but he also did cruel things when he hung out with Pishob and Turik."

"Did he spend a lot of time with them?"

"You mean Pishob and Turik? Yes, they would go somewhere at night. Sneak out after everyone was asleep. Jai never went with them. I don't know if he even knew about their nighttime escapades."

"And you don't know what they did or where they went?" Uri asked.

"No." She looked up at Uri. "Does Rill still hang around Jai?"

"I'm afraid Rill had an accident. He is no longer with us."

"Oh." She put her hand over her mouth." What happened?"

Uri closed his eyes. The guilt and grief whelmed up in him again. "It's a long story. I will tell you sometime."

As they arrived, Uri saw no one was at the docks to meet them. Then he realized it was because no one knew they were coming. A few fishermen hanging around nodded to Coran, and stared at Uri and Aleeta.

"Look, over there." Coran pointed to the farthest dock. "Your father. He must have just come in for the day."

Uri and Coran waved vigorously at him. Elajon stopped and looked at the two men hard. Then recognizing Uri, he dropped the rope and ran towards them. He wrapped his strong arms around Uri and hugged him. Uri noticed he had grown almost as tall as Elajon, not as big or as strong…yet.

Elajon put Uri at arm's length. "Let me look at you. I haven't seen you since we dedicated Ranui. You still dress like a Dombara."

He thought, "*I am a Dombara*," but instead he chose to say, "It's good to see you, Father." This was the first time Uri had called him father.

Elajon's eyes filled with tears. "Bless you, child. Oh, everyone will be so excited to see you." Then he noticed Aleeta. "And who is this?" He held his hand out to welcome her.

"This is Aleeta." Coran introduced her. "She has just gone through a traumatic experience. We are giving her some time to heal, away from her home."

"May our Savior bless you, and welcome to our village." Elajon kissed her cheek. "May you quickly recover here, in our land. Now, everyone, let's go home."

His booming voice swept over them and he put his arm around Uri, leading the way to their small, but comfortable house.

Elajon put his finger on his lips to quiet everyone as he opened the front door. However the fact he came home through the front was enough to alert everyone inside, something was different.

"Look who is here!" he announced joyfully.

Bibbi was the first to fall on Uri. Everyone talking at once caused such an uproar that Aleeta backed out of the door.

"No Aleeta, don't be shy. Come and meet my family." Uri urged. "This is my brother, Bibbi, and my mother." Uri went and hugged her.

Marga fell into her chair and sobbed, holding her apron up to her face. Elajon rolled his eyes.

"This," Uri took Sarella by the hand. "This is my little sister."

Sarella politely nodded, then pulled away.

"Do you remember me?" Uri asked Sarella.

"Oh yes, I remember you." She looked at the floor.

"Wow, she has changed." Uri laughed, recalling the chattering, outgoing child of three.

"She doesn't understand why you weren't happy here and why you didn't like her." Bibbi explained.

"Oh." Stunned, Uri nodded. He really had treated her badly. Pushing her away and refusing her affections.

"Sarella, I am different now. I am happy to see you."

She allowed a smile to play with the corners of her round, pouty mouth. "We'll see." she answered cryptically. She was four and a half now, and seemed to have grown up quite a lot.

Uri turned back to Marga. "Mother," he knelt at her chair. "How would you like to finish fixing dinner for all of us?" He knew the best thing he could ask of her was to cook a big, loving meal. He could smell the stew already simmering in the kitchen.

"Yes, of course." She jumped up. "Come Sarella." Then she stopped and turned to Aleeta. "Would you like to come and help?"

"Thank you, yes I would."

Uri saw the flash of joy in her eyes. This was a good thing, bringing Aleeta with them to this family. It was so full of love and happiness, Aleeta couldn't help but recover. Tomorrow he would take her to see Jai. Maybe she would like to stay with that family for awhile. Uri's heart felt warm and happy. *"The Lord is so good."* he thought.

The next day was a busy one. Aleeta couldn't wait to see Jai, so early in the morning Uri left with Aleeta in tow. He warned her that Jai's family lived in a huge home. Something she had never seen before. However, she wasn't able to understand the immensity of it. When they finally arrived, she was so overwhelmed she didn't want to go up to the door.

"No, it is much too grand for me to even touch the steps. Is his father a ruler or something?"

"No, but he has been blessed with much. When much is given to you, much is required. He is a kind and generous man."

"I could never let Jai see me. He is probably not interested in me anymore."

"Don't be silly." Uri said. "Jai hasn't changed. He lives in here and does not feel it's too grand for him. It's just a house anyway."

"No. It would be better if I never come here again. He has a different life now."

As she spoke, the door opened and Jai came out with Goth behind him, and began running down the stairs. As Jai looked up he stopped in his tracks and his mouth gaped open.

"Aleeta! What are you doing here? Uri, you are here too. Did you bring her, how did you get her away?" The questions spilled out and tumbled over as he gaped in surprise.

"I'm here to see you." she laughed

"Come here and give me a hug." He pointed to his brother. "This is Goth. You must meet my family. Come inside, both of you."

Aleeta hesitated, then taking small steps up to Jai, she held out her hand. Jai grabbed and hugged her. "What a surprise. Come on Uri, come inside."

"No thanks Jai." Uri backed up. Like Aleeta, he felt intimidated by the richness and grandeur, although he would never admit it to anyone. He understood Aleeta's awe of Jai's family stature in the village. "I have some chores to do, and she has a lot to tell you. Send for me when she is ready to come back to my house."

Jai aimlessly waved at Uri and turned his attention back to Aleeta. She did have many things to tell him, not all happy. They needed some time together. Besides, Uri wanted to visit Luwanna. She knew he was here, so it wouldn't be a surprise by any means.

Chapter Thirteen

Kee

Master Tau's mud brick house was a storehouse for various odors. With his head bowed, Kee looked to the dark wall where there were shelves with jars filled with herbs, vials of potions, and baskets overflowed with dried insects and plant roots. On the floor sat tubs of liquids, some with chunks of floating things, bloated and green; a medley of good secrets for healing, and scary secrets for the Spirits to use.

The master's house resided in the shadow of the Bast spiritual temple that towered over the village. The mud bricks that constructed the temple were among the finest, and any leftover bricks became an integral part of the healer, Master Tau's home. Most structures were square; however, the temple was round. That way Spirits could not hide in corners, forcing them to mingle with the people who worshiped them. The design of the temple grew smaller at the top and reached a peak where a flag proudly wafted in the breeze for many years. The flag was bright red, designed to attract any Spirits that happened to be in the area. Kee watched the flag from where he sat, in front of the Master.

Only fully painted Bast men qualified to join the rites in the temple. Women and children sat in rows outside. Kee visualized them sitting in the dark, waving back and forth with the crude music. Soon he wouldn't have to stay with his mother and younger sisters. He could join his father, brothers, and the other men.

Kee prepared for his next step into manhood. He sat before the old Master Tau, the healer, and spiritual leader. For sixteen years, he watched old Tau lead his people. Last year Kee became old enough to began the Shoo rites. For his first mission, Master Tau sent him into the woods to capture the Chola, a great lizard with a vicious bite. It wasn't poisonous, but the wound was nasty and painful. Kee had to catch it without being bitten, and bring it back to the village alive in a wooden cage. This allowed him the right to wear the black marks on his left arm during the Rites of the Spirits, and sit in the front row of the women and children.

The next task took him to the river, where he captured the black eel. That animal was poisonous. Catching it proved his bravery and cunningness. He succeeded, although he almost drowned in the fast moving water of the Bast River.

Kee had looked for the part of the river that ran shallow, where he could walk in and wade over to the area against the bank where the eels hid. Waiting took patience. Within a few hours, he found a small one and grasped its head, just behind the mouth. It was stronger than he expected, and soon he was struggling and slipped into deeper, swifter water. Straining, and gasping for air, he latched onto a branch extruding from the bank and pulled himself, along with the eel, out of the water. He had to take an extra day to recover from this accident. Never telling a soul about the experience, he came back with the dead black eel in his hand, and he earned the right to paint both his arms.

Today his task would be different from the usual rites. He had the honor to perform a special assignment. He felt proud, and sat erect in front of Master Tau with his chest out and his head high. His mother proudly clipped his hair very short this morning. His clear blue eyes sparkled with anticipation.

The sunlight fell into the house through the cracks in the front door. Earlier the old Master shut the windows from prying eyes, for this was a sacred performance. On the third mission, Kee would earn the honor to paint his forehead, and would sit with the men. This rite normally took two missions, but Kee would finish in one.

Kee watched as the Master came toward him. He mumbled something unintelligible, and then sprinkled dust from a dead toad on him. This would help him be a mere shadow in other's eyes.

"Kee, this is your task." Master Tau spoke in their Bast language. "There is a boy your age in the Dombara village. He is a great danger to us and to our way. You are to find him, subdue him, and take him away from all eyes. Warn him not to pursue his plans. Tell him if he continues, harm will come to him and the others he joins with. Then you will cut him and put his blood on this cloth." Tau handed him a small cloth with a figure painted on it. "This figure is a replica of the Spirit Chun. It is powerful medicine. When you have his blood on the cloth, come home, and bring it to me."

Kee breathed deeply. Not expecting to pursue a person, Kee was confused. Shoo Rites were about animals, never people. This would be a difficult test. With hesitation, he accepted the cloth, and stood before his master.

The old man picked up a jar of black paint. He proceeded to mark Kee's arms with short thick strokes. Some curled up, some straight and some pointed down at an angle.

"Master Tau," Kee asked as the painting continued. "How will I find this boy? I do not speak in the Dombara language very well.

"You will do the best you can. He will understand the message you bring. His name is Uri. His cousin is the priest

80

Coran. That is all I can tell you." The old man put down the paint, and muttered a prayer. "Take this."

Kee looked at the weapon in Tau's hand. It was a knife with a wide handle, and a short sharp blade made from the bone of a keymon. This animal had hard thick bones and the Bast used it to make all their knives and spears.

"It is easily hidden." Tau handed it to Kee. "Do this quickly."

"I will bring honor to my people." He bowed deeply before the Master Tau.

Chapter Fourteen

Warning

Uri walked briskly to Luwanna's home. As he approached, he saw Luwanna with several girls in the front yard.

He stood back and watched for a long time. He never felt comfortable with her in this family setting. He didn't understand why. He hoped they could leave, and walk to the play field to talk.

"Hey Uri!" Luwanna ran to him. She hugged him. He was surprised at how much she had grown, and filled out. She was almost fourteen and for once, looked her age. Even as a small infant, she was delicate and frail. Now she looked healthy for the first time. "I heard you were back. Come on, we have a lot to talk about." Luwanna pulled him in the direction of the house.

"Yeh, we have to catch up, but let's walk over to the play field." Uri held on to her.

"You're right. We can be alone. It's easier to talk when we're alone." She grinned and happily skipped down the path, holding his hand.

Uri moved down the path slowly as he listened to Luwanna tell about her recovery from the Getiru attack. He noticed how well her left arm had healed in the last two years. After the attack, it was touch and go whether she would lose it.

Now she could move it around and had regained most of her strength. He still shuddered when he imagined the slain beast before him.

They stopped at the swings and he sat down on one, moving back and forth. Uri noticed the park was empty except for a small group of boys kicking around a cho ball. There he told her about Zekod, and the others. He explained the poisonings, and why the council banished the rest of Zekod's family from the Pinola village.

'I'm here to find Zekod and the other men who escaped from the Pinola Land. That means I have to go to the Bast village." Uri spoke in hushed tones.

"You can't. They will kill you." Luwanna gasped, her eyes opened wide, and she grabbed for his hand.

"Kerka," Uri used her Pinola name affectionately. "There will be quite a few of us. This is something I have to do. I have to talk to Zekod about The Creator."

"Is that why the others are looking for him?"

"No, they will be looking to bring him to justice. He is a murderer." Uri said grimly. "If he only would understand about the forgiveness and love of The Creator..." He turned. There was a noise behind him. He listened. "What was that?"

Luwanna cocked her head. "I didn't hear anything."

Uri got up and walked to the bushes, listening. He motioned for Luwanna to follow him.

As soon as he took the first step into the bushes, he was grabbed by the neck, and thrown to the ground. A foot stepped on his chest, and as he looked up, he saw a boy about his size had Luwanna by the throat. Terror widened her eyes as she struggled to breathe.

"Listen, you forget Zekod." The boy spoke with a broken accent. "We know you and your friends come here to find him" Uri had never heard this accent before. The boy's hair was short, and he wore a type of shoe, not sandals. On his arms were black painted figures.

"Let her go!" Uri yelled as loud as he possibly could, hoping there was someone within earshot.

The shoe-covered foot pushed down harder.

"Remember, you be warned. People die if you don't listen."

Uri saw a flash of a blade, and Luwanna cried out.

"If you hurt her…" Uri struggled harder.

"What will you do?" The boy laughed. "Ah, female blood…bigger magic."

Uri memorized the boy's face as he threw Luwanna to the ground and pressed a cloth against her neck. He turned to Uri, said something in a language Uri wasn't familiar with, and disappeared into the brush behind them.

Uri crawled to Luwanna and saw blood trickle down her throat. "He cut you!"

"Oh," Her hand flew to her throat.

Uri saw terror in her eyes.

She looked at her hand covered in blood.

Uri took off his shirt and pressed it against her neck.

"It's nothing Uri, I'm Okay."

"Hush, I have to stop the bleeding." It took a couple minutes before he had the bleeding under control. They stood up, and Uri wiped away any traces of blood on her throat with his shirt. A tiny puncture revealed where the man cut her. Tiny, but strategically placed where it would be most dramatic.

Furious, he looked from Luwanna to the bushes. "If I ever see him again, that will be his end." Uri threatened.

"No, remember, we are to love our enemies." Luwanna took Uri's face in her hands. Don't seek revenge. I am fine."

Uri took a deep breath. "Well, I guess our mission here is no secret. I must get back and warn Coran." He looked deeply into Luwanna's lovely amber eyes, thick lashes curled up above them.

"Are you sure he didn't hurt you anywhere else? Is your throat okay?"

Luwanna flashed her familiar smile. "Let's go, you can walk me home and then go to Coran.

Don't say anything to anyone else about this, like my family, please. Look to see if any blood is on my dress."

Uri stepped back and examined her clothes. "No, I don't see anything. My shirt is covered, but your dress is fine. Yes, this will be a secret between us." Uri brushed the leaves and dirt off her clothing. He carried his bloody shirt and wore only his vest. "I feel responsible."

Luwanna touched his arm. "Well, you aren't."

They stopped at one of the many fountains in the park and washed her neck, making sure all traces of blood were gone. They turned and went back the way they had entered.

Uri walked with Luwanna all the way to her house. She carried on a conversation as if nothing had happened, but Uri hardly listened. He was fuming inside, blaming himself for allowing them to be surprised by an attacker, and for not gaining the upper hand of the struggle. He could have prevented Luwanna from being hurt if he was stronger and more alert.

Uri vowed never to let a similar situation to occur again. Now he was acutely aware of the animosity of the Bast people, and he would be ever vigilant. Also, he would start carrying a weapon on his person. He thought about what kind of a weapon would be easily hidden in his clothing, yet quickly available. Maybe he would have to make one. As Luwanna chatted, his mind continued to devise and construct something small, but deadly.

Chapter Fifteen

Family

Uri stood in front of the temple. He had never been inside before, but if it was anything similar to the outside, it must be magnificent. He raised and let the knocker drop. It made a resounding "bong" and echoed all around him.

As the door opened a face of a young student appeared. "Yes, may I help you?"

"I am looking for the priest, Coran."

"One moment, please." The boy disappeared into the hollow of the building. It only took a few seconds before Coran ran out to meet Uri.

"Come in, come in."

Uri whispered. "Is there somewhere we can talk, alone?"

"Of course." Coran led Uri down a long hallway and opened a narrow door. "In here." He motioned for Uri to enter the room.

"What is all that blood on your shirt from?" Coran gasped. "Are you alright?"

"Yes, this is Luwanna's blood."

"What happened?"

"She's okay." Uri sat on the bed and looked around. The room contained a single bed, a chair, and a table with a lamp and a couple of books laying on it.

"Is this your bedroom?" Uri asked.

"Yes, this is where I lived while I was a student. This is where I stay when I come here."

"But… you have your own home." Uri stated.

"I live in my parent's home. They gave it to me just before my mother died."

"Oh, your mother, who would have been my aunt, I am sorry. When did she die?"

"Five years ago. My mother had a bad heart. They wanted me to live with them, so they gave me the house with the agreement that they could live in the home as long as they were alive."

Coran changed the subject. "Come on, what happened to Luwanna?"

Uri grew sober. "A while ago, I was walking with her in the park. Someone came up behind us and threw me to the ground, and then he grabbed Luwanna and held a knife to her throat."

"Oh my," Coran sat forward in the chair.

"I think he was a Bast. I'm not sure. His arms were painted with black marks, and he warned me to stop looking for Zekod or we would be killed."

"Those black marks are definitely Bast. Was Luwanna hurt badly?"

"No, I stopped the bleeding, but by telling you this, I am breaking a vow I made to her."

"Well, you have to tell me."

"I know. I think she really meant she didn't want her family to know."

Coran stood up. "This means Zekod is here, but how did they know we came to find him?"

Uri shrugged his shoulders. "Maybe we should keep a low profile, until after the Festival."

"I agree. The Festival of the Full Moons is occurring tonight. I will stay here in the temple for now. Later, I will meet you at the play field with everyone else."

"Good." Uri answered. "I will know where to find you."

"Did Aleeta see Jai yet?"

"Yes, but when she saw where he lived, she was intimidated and didn't want to go."

"What happened?"

"Jai came out as we stood there arguing. He took her in with him. I think she will stay there a while. She will eventually get used to the grandeur."

"She deserves the best." Coran smiled.

"She likes you, very much, you know."

"I like her too."

"Is that all?" Uri asked coyly. "She is a beautiful woman."

"I have other priorities just now. Maybe someday I will pursue that avenue." Coran let a smile dance around the corners of his mouth.

Uri left the temple to walk home, but all the time his mind whirled, consumed with the singular thought of some form of protection. It wasn't for himself. He had to be able to gain the upper hand in the probable event a similar attack should occur in the near future.

Uri rushed into his home with his mind racing. He fantasized of grabbing hold of Zekod and that painted hoodlum who had cut Luwanna. As he stomped into the kitchen and grabbed a piece of fruit from the basket, he heard something that stopped him.

The sound of soft crying came from the back of the house. He put the fruit back and tiptoed down the short hallway to his parent's bedroom. Marga was sitting on the edge of the bed, her face buried in a towel.

"Mother, what's wrong?" Uri asked, and sat next to her on the bed.

"I didn't know anyone was home." She lifted her tear streaked face from the towel. Her face was smooth and unlined for her age. Her hair, light and slightly streaked with grey, was always pulled back, and twisted around the back of her head.

"I just came in." Uri grabbed her hand, soft and small, in his.

"I'm sorry; I miss Tika and the baby."

"Coran will take you over to visit them anytime. You know that."

"Yes, but it's not the same. Oh," she shook her head in frustration. "The women here have their families around them all the time. I miss my family being here, as it used to be. You are gone, Tika is gone." She began to sob again.

Uri wasn't sure what to do. He put his arms around her and held her close, but that seemed to make her cry more. "Mother... Tika and Koori are doing what The Creator wants them to do. I'm sure we can work something out so you can see each other and the baby more often. I'll talk to Father and..."

"No, don't say anything to Elajon. He thinks I am too emotional."

"Can I talk to Coran about it?"

She sniffed and blew her nose into the towel. "Yes, that would be alright."

Uri wiped the tears from her face. "Now go wash up and get ready for tonight. We are going to have a good time tonight." He tried to cheer her up.

"Yes, of course." she answered. "I wonder what Tika and Koori will be doing?" She began to cry again. He certainly didn't want to tell her they would be hiding in caves, away from the rest of the tribe, because of the rites to the Evil Spirits.

Uri, maintaining a happy face, steered her thoughts to her other children. "How about getting up and making Bibbi and Sarella a snack before we go to the play field."

"Yes, I must be ready for them."

They could now hear the voices of the children as they came in from playing on the rope swing in the backyard. She wiped her face and hands on the apron she always wore, and headed for the kitchen.

Uri breathed a sigh of relief. He hoped he thought to say the right things. He didn't know much about his mother. She always stayed in the background while Elajon cast a large shadow around his family.

Chapter Sixteen
Celebration

The darkening sky was clear. It was at the end of the dry months, and the days were usually very warm with clear skies. Tonight, excitement among those gathered at the play field was infectious. Uri sat on the ground beside his ten-year-old brother Bibbi, while Coran and Aleeta sat directly behind. The rest of the family, friends, and neighbors, were scattered about while they waited, holding their collective breath. Uri was unable to curb his impatience. He got up, walked about, and then sat down again.

"Fidgeting isn't going to make it happen any faster." Marga called out.

He grinned at her.

Then it began. Low in the eastern sky, only a few degrees apart, two golden orbs poked up from behind the hills. The moons, Venca and Visca ascended into the night sky, completing the two hundred-year cycle. The twin moons were full, at the same time. The light blocked all the stars and made the night glow, as if the sun had begun to rise.

All who gathered took a deep breath, and expressed their awe with silence. Moments passed as the moons climbed higher, until they hung in the sky, side by side. It was a phenomenal glimpse of the majesty of The Creator.

Pujim, the Chief of the Dombara tribe stood in front of the crowd. "Look at the glory that The Creator of All has given to us."

Cheers and hoops of joy broke the spell.

Luwanna, with her golden hair tied at the side, Dombara style for young maidens, ran over to the area where Uri and his family sat. She plopped herself down directly in front of Uri.

"Whatcha think of that?" she asked, with rampant enthusiasm.

"Pretty spectacular." Uri nodded.

"Aren't we blessed to be alive when this occurred?"

"Yes, we certainly are."

Bibbi edged closer to Uri. "Luwanna, why don't you get lost?"

"Bibbi," gasped Marga. "That's rude. You have been very rude to people lately"

Luwanna stood up and wrinkled her nose at Bibbi, then waved at Uri. "Bye, for now."

The crowd began to thin, and Uri with his family made their way to the Dombara's Meeting House that was in the same complex as the temple, where a grand feast had been prepared for the night of celebration. All the children, kidnapped from Pinola Land, ended up in this same large room when they first arrived in the Dombara Land. It was the first building they saw.

Uri held Sarella's hand. He had tried the last few days, to make up to her. She slowly came around, and her old self peeked out as she chattered away. She was so different from her brother, Bibbi. Where he was quiet and to the point, she could talk for an hour about how the trees swayed in the breeze or how many stars she could see in the heavens.

Jai ambled up as they approached the building, and took Sarella from Uri, hoisting her up on his shoulders. She squealed with glee. Jai was very tall, and his golden hair, pulled back in a braid, swung back and forth. All males in the tribe began wearing a braid at the age of fourteen. Until then hair grew long, and curled around their faces, like Bibbi.

"Doesn't take much to make her happy." Uri said.

"Nope." Jai bounced her along. He looked around for Aleeta.

Uri gestured to the building in front of them. "Aleeta is with Coran. They ran ahead. You never sent her back."

"She has been staying with us." Jai said. "I think my parents are going to ask her to stay permanently."

"That would be wonderful for her. I don't think she wants to go back to Pinola Land. She has nothing there anymore."

"How long will you be able to stay?"

"School starts in three weeks. Suwat and Beka won't miss me. They are busy with their businesses and doing very well. Suwat has made a good living constructing pens for the ovis, and making nets. As for Beka, she knows how to sell anything. She has her garden and her stall at the Marketplace."

"Good, maybe we will have time to talk." Jai looked serious. "Aleeta told me everything about Zekod and the rest. Can't say I feel sorry about their banishment. When are you going over to the Bast area?"

"I'm not sure."

Inside the dining room, people were bustling around, scrambling to get everyone served at the many tables. Uri's

94

family ambled over to an empty table where their families and friends could gather. Jai and his brothers sat at the table next to Uri. Luwanna's older sister, Lyshon squeezed in next to Goth, and Uri noticed they held hands as the head priest Elari, offered the blessing over the food.

When the blessing was over Luwanna ran up to Uri and whispered in his ear, "They're in love." She giggled and ran off again.

A strong voice rose over the din. "Listen everyone...Jinela is going to play."

A lovely young woman, a little older than Tika, sat in front of the room with the four-string instrument on her lap. Her skin was the color of milk and her long deft fingers began to strum as she hummed softly. The tune was haunting. Then she raised her head and her voice sang loud and strong:

> "Our Creator signed His name across the skies,
> and revealed His majesty to our feeble eyes.
> How mighty is His Name?
> We must look in awe and realize
> We creatures are foolish and lame.
> He alone... He alone is wise."

Uri listened in awe at the performance. He had never heard anything so beautiful. He could listen to her forever, but as she finished Uri's attention diverted to a young man moving toward the group. Uri whispered to Bibbi, "Who is that?"

Bibbi whispered back. "His name is Oden. His mother was Dombara and his father a Mudan. He's considered a member of the tribe only because his mother lived in our village."

Oden stood at Jai's table and next to Lyshon and Goth. "Good evening everyone. Are all of you enjoying yourselves tonight?"

Uri thought he behaved stiffly, and his real reason for greeting them was more than a friendly hello, so Uri motioned to an empty chair. "Come, sit down."

"Thank you, I believe I will… for a moment."

Just as Uri was about to ask him some questions Elajon came up and put his hands on Marga's shoulders.

"Hello everyone. Sorry I couldn't join you on the play field, but being on the serving committee, I had to stay here. We watched from the front of the building. What an inspirational sight."

He picked up a biscuit and took a bite out of it. "Oh by the way, I just heard that the Bast tribe plans to participate at the Marketplace the day after tomorrow."

"Oh really." Marga replied. "We had better stay home then."

"Now stop being so nervous. You always worry for nothing." He scolded his wife.

Uri perked up. "What's the problem with the Bast being at the market?" he asked.

"Every time they come, something bad happens." Marga said.

"No, that's not really true." Elajon explained. "It seems that way. Their attitude aggravates many people, so everyone is on edge when they show up. However, they always bring things that sell well; fruits that we don't grow here, beautiful furniture pieces and other wood products. They specialize in wood carved from the Tangleroot Tree. They also have medicinal products that many people stock up on, so they are really an asset."

Marga shook her head and sighed. "We have to put up with them."

Uri was about to ask about the medical products when Bibbi piped up.

"Good," Bibbi said. "We can get some of the fruit I like."

Oden broke in, "The Bast culture is inferior to ours. Their ways are very different, strange, and they are pagans. They worship the creation, not The Creator. These moons becoming full tonight, they have superstitions about those things. Many people fear them because of those superstitions. When they come to the market, they price their things higher than they need too. In my opinion, they are not very civilized. In fact they are backwards and barbaric."

"You sound a little prejudiced." Goth nudged his friend.

"Not at all. As you know, I have observed their mannerisms and customs at a close proximity. I don't believe they should be allowed into our village."

Uri listened closely.

Elajon admonished Oden. "I understand why you feel that way, but you know as well as I, that The Creator made all men in His image. It will help if you look at them through the eyes of the Savior."

Uri looked at his Father with astonishment. Elajon had been told why Coran brought Uri along and what they had to do. Elajon was aware of the crimes the Bast helped Zekod commit. Still, Elajon seemed to be defending them.

"Yes, The Creator made the Bast people, but they give all the credit to the Evil One. That's who they worship." Oden said with scorn.

"Nevertheless," Elajon said, looking at Uri. "They will be there. The committee has approved it."

"Well, this looks like that market day will be very interesting." Uri speculated.

"I'm not sure interesting is the right word to use." Elajon replied.

Chapter Seventeen
The Dengu Plant

He was old, having seen many years in this area of the forest. However, tonight he felt a vague apprehension in his bones. There was a strange smell to the night air. His ears, scarred from many combats, twitched. His nose, not as sensitive as it had been in his younger days, tilted up, sniffing. Still, he was acutely aware of the odors drifting up.

Once those odors passed his scent glands, and deciphered by his brain, he knew what was edible and inedible, where it was safe, and where danger lurked. He knew who and where his enemies were.

The old getiru was hoping to come across his favorite food, a hoperl, a small, hairless creature with large pointed ears, and a long tail. Hoperls lived in holes near the roots of many trees in the area. They were easy to catch, and did not take much energy to kill and devour. Tonight he had seen not even one.

It was painful to make his way through the brush, but he was in no hurry. When tired, he would sit back on his haunches and rest. His bright eyes, sitting close on his wide bony face, missed nothing in the surrounding forest. The bumps on his head, with large holes serving as ears, funneled in every rustle or unusual sound. Padding through the deepest part of the forest, nothing seemed out of place as he passed beneath the Dengu plant, and came to a clearing. Still, he knew instinctively, this night was different.

He stopped and looked up into the unusually bright night sky. It was a view he had never seen before. In place of the partial twin lights, two bright, round orbs gleamed down into his black eyes. As he sat looking into the sky, he noticed a mist rise up, growing thicker by the second, enshrouding that rare jewel, the Dengu plant. The getiru knew this plant was "The Queen of the Forest."

The fur, striped orange and black, bristled in alertness as he gazed up the thick stock of the Dengu plant. It grew to a great height among the surrounding Tangleroot trees, and as he watched, the Dengu's golden leaves shimmered in the bright light of the twin orbs.

His nose began to twitch, and the ear stubs on top of his head worked back and forth.

From above, he saw the large golden leaves shudder, and thousands of spores floated down to the forest floor. Curious, he backed up and lingered, watching the Dengu spores reach and infiltrate the ruby-colored fruit of the nearby Cheekee tree.

As the fruit accepted the spores, a pervasive stench reached his nostrils. The old cat felt the fur rise high on the back of his scrawny neck, and a soft growl escaped from him. He sensed something evil had occurred. Instinctively he bounded away from the area, encasing himself in the dense foliage. He looked back and a shudder traveled through his long body.

The getiru continued his night prowl. However, he made sure he stayed clear from any area where he sensed the Dengu existed.

Chapter Eighteen
The Marketplace

The three men and two women were busy in the booth where the Bast people usually set up their wares. Uri watched and decided that they definitely were different. It was the prime market area, and many venders wanted to have the opportunity to occupy it. However, when the Bast came they demanded that very spot. Since they brought in a huge amount of customers, they always got what they wanted.

Uri sat on a bench close to the main area, studying them as they moved about in their booth. The men wore their hair cropped close to their scalps, but the women's hair was long and they piled it high on the top of their head and tied a bright colored scarf around it. Their clothing was from animal skins made into vests, and they wore a light gauzy shirt under it. On their feet, they wore shoes, not sandals. The women wrapped a multi-colored cloth around their bodies, and topped that with a furry sweater-like wrap. They chatted back and forth in a language strange to Uri's ears.

On the back of one of the women was a sling with a baby, snug deep inside. The women also pierced their ears and noses with shiny jewels, and their lips were tattooed black. Uri looked hard, but none of them had any marks on their arms. The three men consistently stopped people as they past and urged them to examine their goods, while the women sat and cooked. One was making a pancake, frying it, and folding it down the middle, then slapped a spoonful of juicy looking meat on it.

'Hey," Jai sat down on the bench beside Uri. "Guess what kind of meat the Bast women are cooking?"

"I don't have any idea."

"It's a black eel, from the Bast River. It's the only place the eel lives. I hear it is good."

"Why don't you buy some?" Uri joked. "Maybe it tastes like a wona." He referred to the Pinola's delicious worm that lived under the sand on the dunes.

"I will, if you will."

Uri grinned. "What else do they have over there?"

"They sell three different kinds of fruit, medicinal herbs, and roots. Can you see the wooden bowls? They make them from the Tangleroot tree that grows in their land. They usually have furniture too, but I didn't see any this time."

Uri could see Elajon in the distance with his brother Kinter, Coran's father. They had brought in fish earlier this morning, and sold all of it to the fishmongers. Now they seemed to be shopping. He turned his attention back to Jai. "Where's the rest of your family?"

"They didn't come today. There is a big meeting with Lyshon's family. I think wedding plans are in the future."

"Isn't she a bit young?"

"No, she's seventeen. By the time the planning is done and the wedding day arrives, she'll be eighteen."

"My sister Tika got married at eighteen."

"That's right. How are they doing, over in the Pinola village?"

"Great, they have established a good following of The Creator, and hold meetings every week, as we do here. Also they have increased their family." Uri smiled. "They have a baby boy named Ranui. There hasn't been a baby in the Pinola village for what… seven years?

"That will give them hope."

"They desperately need hope."

Bibbi ran up, out of breath and interrupted the conversation. "Hi, Sarella and mother are coming. Let's go and buy some fruit."

"You are interrupting us. That is rude." Uri scolded.

"I'm sorry."

"Just like with Luwanna, you were rude to her."

"Well… Luwanna wants to take all your time, and I haven't had a chance to talk with you at all."

"Are you jealous of Luwanna?"

"I don't like her." Bibbi pouted.

"Did you know when she lived in the Pinola village her family ignored her and treated her very badly. She went hungry most of the time. You should be happy for her. Now she is with a loving family."

Bibbi grunted. Uri could see a lot of his former self in Bibbi.

As he scowled at his younger brother, Sarella ran up with a breathless Marga close behind.

She wiped her brow. "I can hardly keep up with these youngsters."

"Come on, let's go." Sarella hopped up and down with excitement. Bibbi was off and running with his sister, leaving the rest to trail behind.

They went up to the Bast enclosure. Bibbi picked through the several ruby colored fruit in the basket. "Can we have one Mother?"

"Oh, they are more expensive than last time. I don't think so."

"How about you and Sarella sharing one?" Uri offered.

"That's okay with me." Bibbi looked for the biggest one and Uri pulled out a small pocketknife, cutting the chosen fruit in half. The flesh was as red as the outer skin and a small pocket of seeds lay close to the stem. He handed a half to each child.

"This is Cheekee." The Bast man said, staring at Uri. "Picked yesterday, very fresh."

Uri recognize the accent. It was just like to boy's accent who had attacked him and Luwanna. As Uri handed the Bast man the coins he looked into his ice blue eyes. A cold, nasty chill penetrated straight through him. Uri discerned evil in this man. Since his encounter with the boy, who certainly was Bast, he believed the whole tribe must be the same.

As he turned, Uri saw the two children greedily devouring the fruit. "Hey, you didn't leave any for the rest of us to taste."

Bibbi wiped his mouth on the bottom of his shirt, much to Marga's dismay. "Nope."

"You want to buy another?" The Bast spoke softly, with a ghost of a smile.

"I think not." Uri walked away. He wanted to leave these people behind.

It was late afternoon and time for the family meeting and worship. Before prayer, Elajon sat straight in his chair, and looked directly at Bibbi.

"Tell me, what is the reason for this rudeness you have been exhibiting the last few weeks?"

"I don't know." Bibbi said.

"You were always such a sweet little boy." Marga whimpered.

"Quiet, Mother." Elajon said gently. "That doesn't help."

Uri spoke up. "He told me he didn't like Luwanna, because when I came to visit she took up too much of my time."

"I realize you are growing up." Elajon addressed Bibbi. "There is a difference between feeling grown up and actually being mature. Perhaps you need to realize you are still a child. Remember the manners we taught you, and respect your elders. It is an important part of accepting your place in our society."

"Yes, Father." Bibbi was obviously remorseful. "I don't know why I want to be mean, it just comes out."

"Well young man, just keep it in." Elajon shook his head. "Are we ready for prayer now?"

"May I pray first?" Bibbi asked.

"Of course." Elajon replied.

Uri hoped the old Bibbi was back, and remembered how he occasionally tested Beka when he was that age. Bibbi had a good heart and a pure spirit. He would be fine. Uri felt so grateful that he could watch his little brother grow. He knew

The Creator had wonderful plans for Bibbi, or Bright Dawn, his ancient name.

Chapter Nineteen
Life or Death

Bibbi watched Uri turn off the lantern. The only light in the room came from the moons, now losing their fullness at different stages.

Bibbi sat on the edge of his bed. "Remember the first time we saw each other?"

"Sure, on the dunes in Pinola Land. You came right up to me, while I was holding the grag in my hand. You were either brave or stupid."

They laughed as Bibbi bounced on his bed. "I wasn't brave. I was curious." He turned thoughtful. "It's been less than two years, but so much has changed."

"If I had stayed here in Dombara, and not tried to sail back," Uri mused. "Rill would not have drowned, and the Pinolas would never have heard the Word of the Savior."

"Rill was not a good person, but I'm sorry he died." Bibbi yawned. "What are we doing tomorrow?"

"I have to meet with Coran sometime during the day. We must begin to plan how to find Zekod."

"Can we spend some time at the play field together?"

"Sure." Uri stretched and tried not to think about the task ahead. "Goodnight… little brother."

"Good night... big brother."

***

Bibbi woke with a pain in his head and his stomach. He tried to sit up in bed, but the room began to spin. He felt so sick. He never felt sick before. Maybe a little tummy-ache from eating too much, but this was very bad. If he could get to the toilet, or get a drink of water it might help. But the toilet was outside, and the water in the kitchen. Bibbi knew he would never make it to the door.

He called out to Uri. "I don't feel good. Would you get me a drink, please?"

Uri sat up, Bibbi saw him rub his eyes. "What's the matter?"

"I don't know. My stomach and head hurt."

Uri came over and looked at him, then felt his head. "You feel awfully warm."

"Everything is spinning around. I feel so sick."

"Lay down and I'll get Mother." Bibbi watched as Uri went out the door. He shut his eyes and then… nothing.

Uri hurried down the hall and saw Marga in Sarella's room. The lantern mapped soft designs on the walls.

"What's the matter with Sarella?" Uri began to feel alarmed.

"She's feeling sick."

"So is Bibbi."

By now, Elajon was up and at the doorway. "Who's sick?"

"Sarella and Bibbi."

"What seems to be wrong?"

"Bibbi said his stomach and head hurt."

"Sarella said the same." Marga said.

Elajon looked at Sarella as she lay moaning in her bed, then looked at Bibbi.

Elajon yelled down the hall. "He's unconscious. Mother put Sarella in Uri's bed so she is in the same room with Bibbi. I'm going for the Ajaben." He threw on his coat and rushed out the door.

Uri helped Marga rearrange the room so both children were together. He had Marga gather towels, water and some medicinal herbs they had for stomachaches. Uri purposely gave her chores to do to keep her busy, and less likely to panic. His mother was a loving woman, but not good in a crisis.

He sat on the edge of Bibbi's bed and shook him gently, "Come on, wake up."

Bibbi opened his eyes and mumbled something, then shut them again.

"Here's some water." Marga handed Uri a cup, half full.

"Bibbi, here is some water. You said you wanted water."

He leaned forward and Uri held the cup to his mouth. Most of it ran down onto his chest.

Marga turned, "Oh, I hear Elajon." She ran down the hall.

Elajon came into what now had become the sick room. Ajaben, the doctor and priest, sat on the edge of the bed next to Uri and examined Bibbi. Then he went over to Sarella.

"It looks like what I have been seeing all night."

"What is it?" Elajon asked.

"I'm not sure, but a have a suspicion. If I am right... we need to have a tribal meeting now, immediately. This is turning into an emergency."

***

Everyone, frightened and anxious, came together in the Meeting Hall. It was crowded and some people had to gather at the doorways. The sun began to announce the arrival of a new day as the meeting began. At the head table sat Pujim, Ajaben, Coran, and Ando, Jai's father. Pujim stood up and motioned for quiet.

"Listen, please." He waited. "We are facing a crisis. Several children and a few adults seem to be ill. We think we know what is happening, but we want to ask if anyone here bought and ate the cheekee fruit the Bast people brought to the Marketplace?"

"My daughter bought some and she is sick."

"I bought some too, my children are sick." another added.

Several people stood and told how their children or relatives had bought, eaten some, and how sick they were now.

"The evidence points to the fruit. Anyone who ate all, or part of the fruit, is now sick. No one that is here ate any of it. Is that true?"

"Yes, yes."

110

"What does that mean?" Someone in the back of the room shouted. Murmurs began to circulate.

Ajaben stood and raised his hands for quiet.

A loud cry rose up accusing the Bast for purposely poisoning the tribe. Ajaben again motioned for quiet. "No, the Bast didn't poison the fruit. Listen to me." He waited until everyone sat back down. Uri knew the tribe trusted these four men and would give them a chance to explain.

"I need to tell you a legend concerning the fruit from the cheekee tree. It is a very old legend, and many of you have never heard even part of it. A few nights ago, we experienced a wondrous sight. Our moons became full simultaneously. The legend goes like this... 'The leaves are long and wide, a golden color and it grows very high. It is the Dengu Plant, our Queen of the Forest. Be careful my friends, for beauty can be deadly when moons grow large. Our queen will quiver with evil delight, and releases her gift to any ruby fruit that reaches for it.' "

Audible whispers began to circulate again, all around the room.

"Every two hundred years, when the moons rise and they are full, the leaves of the Dengu release spores that float to the ground. It propagates that way. However, if the cheekee trees nearby are producing fruit at that time, the spores melt into the fruit and its flesh becomes poison. The Dengu is rare and not many exist, so the Cheekee bearing fruit near the Dengu plant at this particular time would be unusual.

"This is a very old legend and no one really believed it, probably because no one has ever seen it happen. Now we know it is true. We know the Bast people harvested the fruit after the full moons, and brought it to market to sell. They only brought a few. Maybe they suspected something, maybe they didn't. I doubt if they knew if it was poisoned. They might not

111

have even checked to see if any Dengu's were in the area. The important thing is we need to find an antidote."

Oden rose and spoke loudly. "If this is the poison the Bast uses to capture animals for food I believe there is an antidote."

A loud cry rose from those gathered.

"Quiet!" called out Pujim. He waited until order resumed. "It is hard for us to know what is true and what is myth. Two hundred years is a long time. If the Bast collected the poison two hundred years ago, why would they have any left?'

"They have barrels of the poison and they use very little. They may not know where that poison came from." Coran said.

"And maybe they do." A voice from the back of the room shouted.

Again, everyone began accusing the Bast tribe of purposely using the poison against them.

Coran stood, "It doesn't make any sense why they would harm us. Besides, we can't accuse them unless we know for sure. But if there is an antidote, we need to go to the Bast people and buy it."

Oden rose again. "I doubt if you will be able to get into their village before being driven back. They aren't friendly."

"We know that." Pujim waved his remark away with his hand.

"If this antidote exists, and they refuse to sell us any, we will have to get it another way." Oden persisted.

"We must try. Doctor, tell us how much time we have." Pujim said.

Ajaben stood and slowly looked around the room. Suddenly there was absolute silence. "The coma will last for a time, maybe weeks…"

Before he could finish, a loud wail circled the room. Emotionally, they flailed about, trying to cope with this new and terrifying experience. It was many moments before order crept back and settled into the room.

"Please," Ajaben pleaded. "Don't panic. We need to find the antidote if it exists, and we will."

"We don't want the Bast at our Marketplace again!" shouted a large, angry man.

"Don't be hasty." Pujim cautioned. "We have no facts as to who is involved or how this happened. The Bast offer many products we need, and they must sell them to us for the good of their community. Let's not cut off the relationship before we have all the facts." His logic seemed to work. The people calmed down.

Someone in the back of the room raised their hand and stood. "How do you propose to get this antidote? The Bast may not give it to us. We don't have any assurance anyone can even get to the village."

"What will happen if there isn't an antidote? Will everyone who is sick die?" The question circulated around the room.

Goth stood. "We will find something, and we will get it. We can't go right into their village and ask for it. That will never work. We have to be clever. There are plenty of us to figure a way. Be assured of that."

Uri looked around. This was a great dilemma. However, he knew it was possible to do. Besides, they had to apprehend Zekod in any case. There was a two-fold reason to sneak into Bast territory (three… if you count his desire to catch up with the painted boy who hurt Luwanna.)

Chapter Twenty
Travel Plans

Pujim did not want to break the meeting up until everyone understood. He wanted more details of the emergency. He motioned for Oden to stand and relate his knowledge.

"I have seen animals in this state." Oden said. "The Bast people collect and keep them for weeks. This poison actually keeps the animals in good condition until they want to slaughter one. If they capture several at once, they don't have to hunt often. They collect keymons, getirus, and even lizards that way."

"I have never seen a keymon. What do they look like?" Pujim asked.

"A furry animal that lives in the forest, stands about this tall." Oden explained, and lowered his hand to his waist. "It has a long tail and swings by it from tree to tree."

Uri began to wonder how this man Oden knew so much about the Bast and their customs.

A man in front asked, "How long can the animals be kept in this coma state?"

"Several weeks if they take care of them. They have young boys rub them down with water and keep them clean." Oden said.

"How can we take care of our family members who are infected?" A woman asked

Oden raised his hand for silence. "If you keep forcing fluids into them, they will be okay for weeks."

Coran added. "During this time it seems a person takes a breath every minute or so, and their pulse is very slow. Maybe they can hear you. If you ask them to open their mouth, they may obey, and fluids can be given to them. You will have to try everything you can think of."

"Keep them warm and in a dark room. Massage their arms and legs often and talk to them as much as you can." Oden added.

"We propose five young men volunteer to travel into the Bast territory and do what they must to get the antidote, if there is one." Pujim's countenance became stern. "This is an extremely dangerous mission. Not only would you be facing menacing forests, treacherous rivers, savage animals, but also suspicious, aggressive people. On top of everything else, there is a time element."

Uri didn't think twice. His hand rose immediately. Goth, Jai and Coran's hands went up at the same time.

A smug look crept across Oden's face. "You need me to guide you."

Everyone seemed to agree.

"Why you?" asked Uri. He was having a hard time liking this man.

"He is right, Uri. He can guide us and show us the way." Goth spoke quietly.

"Fine, then it is settled. The five of you will leave as soon as possible. You have only a few days to complete your task and get back home." Pujim said. "Now everyone go home, and tend to the sick. Find a way to get fluid into their bodies."

"All of you meet me at my house." Goth said to the other four. "We will pack what we need and lay plans for traveling."

"If we leave before noon, we could arrive at the Bast River by nightfall." Oden looked at Uri.

"Why does he always stare at me?" Uri thought. *"As if he didn't trust me, or was hiding something from me."*

Oden was short and wide, very muscular. He took after his Mudan father, with a curved, full facial structure. His round eyes protruded like pools of liquid brown. Nothing like the Dombaras or Pinolas, who shared sharp, chiseled features, and orange to dark amber colored eyes. Oden stood out among them. Maybe that was why he behaved with self-assuredness, including a smack of pretentiousness. He knew he was different.

Uri followed the young men out into the cool dawn. Jai and Goth lead the way.

From nowhere Luwanna came running. "Uri wait." Breathlessly she stood in front of them.

"Uri take me along. I'm small and can do things and get into places you men can't."

"No way." Uri shook his head.

"Please, I really can help."

"I know you want to help us, but you would be in the way. We would be distracted trying to keep you safe. This is a dangerous trip and we only have a few days."

"It's just because I'm a girl. You told me before. You wouldn't take me on the dunes because I'm a girl."

"No. You can't come." Uri turned and left her behind.

***

Luwanna watched as the men disappeared down the path. She wasn't sure if she felt angry or hurt. However, nothing would stop her from helping. She knew that in the depth of her being, she must follow them. She walked to her home the back way, and slid into the bedroom from the back door.

Looking around, she tried to decide what to pack for the trip. She would need something for a shelter, food, and water. Also, the leaves she chewed for pain in her bad arm. In a few moments, her backpack began to bulge. Luwanna hoped her handicapped arm would not slow her down, or hinder in keeping up with the men, but she had become a good tracker, thanks to Jai and Goth, and continued to climb trees, her favorite past time. She believed all those activities would help her stay on their trail. Satisfied with the necessities she had packed, she wrote a short message to her mother.

Mother, I am following the men to help. Don't worry. If I find I can't keep
up, or if I think I am getting in over my head, I will come back. I am
smarter than you think and I know my way around the woods...
Love to you, Father, Lyshon, and little Darv. Luwanna
She smiled at the thought of her three-year-old brother. Luwanna had become very close to him.

She placed the note on her pillow, hoisted the pack onto her back, and slipped out the back door. Luwanna knew the first phase of the trek. It was down the well-used path from the back of the village, through the scattering of trees, and down to the edge of the forest. At that point, the paths broke up, and she would wait, hidden until they came by. She would watch in which direction they continued. She was physically strong and mentally determined. At the end, she believed Uri would be glad she came.

Chapter Twenty-One

Oden

Uri looked back at Luwanna as she walked away. He prayed she wouldn't try anything foolish. Coran fell in step with Uri, but Oden lagged behind. They climbed the steps, and began down the path that lead to Jai and Goth's home when Oden called out.

"Uri, may I speak with you?" Both Coran and Uri turned, looking back. "Alone, please." Oden added.

"I'll catch up with you." Uri said to Coran.

Oden began. "I would like to be friends. You may not realize, but you are a hero to many of the Dombaras. I know about the kidnappings. I know you all became the Pinola's children, brought up in the Pinola land. It must have been a shock for you all to find out who your real families were."

"That's hardly the word for it." Uri said.

"I saw how the returning children, from the Pinola tribe, struggled with who they really were and their adjustment to life here. I heard you ran away, and got lost at sea. Then Coran found you on that sand bar. Everyone was overjoyed at your conversion, and how you finally brought the Good News and hope back to the Pinolas. That is the miracle everyone had been praying for."

They began walking slowly, following the others. Oden continued. "I am familiar with your story and history; however you do not know me."

Uri was irritated with this jabber. "So what's your point?"

"I too was kidnapped. I was six. I was kidnapped by the Bast, after they killed my father in front of me."

Uri stopped and looked wide-eyed at Oden.

"I am not telling you this to shock you, but since everyone except you knows my story, I think you need to hear it."

As Oden began, Uri moved close beside him, and listened.

"My father was a Mudan and a hunter. Usually he brought the tribe small animals and birds. On that day, he took me into the forest to teach me to shoot the slether, a type of sling. His choice of weapons was the spear, but all Mudans learned the slether."

Uri thought of the grag he used on the dunes to kill the wona. All Pinola boys learned to use that weapon.

Oden continued. "We hadn't gone far into the forest when he spotted the footprints of a large male outnu."

"What's that?"

"An animal about four foot high, with four legs, long head, and a short white tail. It has brown fur and in the autumn, the males grow a bony outcrop on their skulls. They use it to fight for the females. It is very good meat, and a large one, like he saw, would feed the whole village. If he could kill it and get it home, he would gain stature among his people. They shunned him because he married a Dombara, and this could repair the estrangement. So, he began to track it. He was a very good tracker, one of the best. We traveled for hours. I remember

121

being very tired. Late in the afternoon, he looked around and told me we had entered Bast territory, and be very quiet. He would not let the animal get away. He felt that since he had tracked it, the outnu belonged to him."

"Then it came into a clearing. He had a clear shot. He aimed and the spear went through the heart, and it dropped dead on the spot. Instantly Bast men surrounded us. They looked frightening, especially to a small boy. Black marks on their faces and arms, holding spears aimed at us, and piercing angry ice blue eyes. They told my father in their accent that the outnu was theirs and we were trespassing. We must immediately turn and leave. My father refused and the arguing grew loud. He gestured with his spear and someone must have thought he was going to attack. Two men speared him, like the outnu, through the heart".

"He dropped dead at my feet. They began to talk angrily among themselves. Overcome with shock and grief, I don't remember much after that".

"They took me to an old woman, and I stayed with her three years. She was kind and I learned many things from her. I learned their way of thinking, their language, and their culture. I could find my way around their land and knew it well. After those three years passed, she died."

"Again I felt that terrible grief and fear. Two Bast men dragged me into the woods, over the river, and left me near the Mudan village. I think they were the ones who killed my father".

"I stumbled into that village, now nine years old. After they heard my story, they took me to my mother, who now had gone back to her people in the Dombara village. I never forgot all I had learned about the Bast." He hesitated. "The vision of my mother is still clear in my mind. She ran to me. I wasn't sure at the time who she was. Then when she took me in her

122

arms and her tears fell on my face, I vaguely remembered living a happy life in the Mudan village."

"I went home with her to an unfamiliar hut with grandparents I didn't know. However, it wasn't long before life took on a routine. I went to school with the other boys and girls. However, it was there I learned clearly, I was not one of them. I was not a Dombara or a Mudan, and definitely not a Bast. I wondered who I was, and I began to hate the Bast for contorting my world into a twisted mess. It took many years before I came to terms with who I was."

Uri could tell Oden believed he was unique. The knowledge of the Bast society made him invaluable to the Dombaras, and he became a go-between with the Mudans, but the Uri sensed the hatred continued for his father's killers. He thought he cleverly buried it under a plethora of controlled beliefs and facts.

"Hatred is a very ugly thing." Uri said.

"I had to learn to overcome it. However, I do not trust the Bast people or want them anywhere in our village."

"Are they really as fierce as you say?" Uri questioned Oden.

"Yes."

"So you are going with us, because you can help us find what we are looking for, but also to put one over on them." Uri smiled.

"I am helping my tribe, the Dombaras. The Bast are ruthless and savage. I know you and Coran are here to find that man who bought the poison from them to hurt your people in the Pinola village. They know what their poisons can do. I believe they sold the fruit here, knowing it was poisoned."

123

Oden smiled. "I have unique knowledge of their land and of them."

"Thank you for sharing the story with me, Oden. I understand you much better now, and I think we can be friends."

***

As Oden explained himself and his life, Uri tasted fear rise up in his throat. He thought of the attack on himself and Luwanna. What had he gotten himself into? Uri wasn't the bravest of his companions, and often jumped into the fire before he thought about it. However, Bibbi and Sarella's lives depended on the success of this mission. He had to swallow the fear and trust in the mercy of The Savior. He hoped his faith was as strong as it would need to be.

They arrived at the stately home and Jai waved them up the steps. "Hey you two, hurry.

We need to get going."

Inside the home, everyone had gathered in the dining area.

"Does anyone know what we are looking for?" Goth asked.

"No, but we have a contact." Coran said.

"Who? Is it a Bast?" Uri was surprised.

"Yes," Coran looked at Uri. "That was what I didn't want to tell you. Oden and I know a Bast who has been helping us. He understands the problems and made contact with us a few months ago. He brought me the antidote for the poisonings. I hoped we could have him meet us at the river. However, it is risky and we may have to cross it without his help."

"Once we are in the area of the village, we can go to his home, and find where they store the materials." Oden added.

While discussing the necessary supplies, Lyshon entered. She had been in the kitchen with Jai and Goth's mother, Ferra. Lyshon listened for a few minutes, but Uri could tell she was agitated.

"Goth did you know Frash is also sick?"

"No," Both brothers stood up alarmed. "When did he eat the fruit?"

"I guess it was only a bite, from one of his friends."

She leaned on the table next to Goth. "Why do you have to go. Sending Jai is enough sacrifice from one family."

"I must go." Goth said.

"No, you don't have to go. You want to go."

"Fine, then I want to go." They scowled at each other.

"Don't I mean more to you?" She stood up, and put her hands on her hips. "We have a wedding to plan."

"This is more important than a wedding. It's life or death for many people."

"But it might be death for you, please don't go." Lyshon sat down and began to cry.

"Um..." Goth looked at everyone at the table. "Can I have a few minutes, alone?"

"Just a few, then we need to go." Oden admonished.

In the next room, Uri and the rest tried not to listen to the loud voices. Embarrassed, they all shuffled their feet and looked aimlessly around. When Goth waved them back, he looked ashen. "She has ended our engagement. She will understand later."

They all could hear Lyshon in the kitchen sobbing something to Ferra.

Oden took a no nonsense approach. "Now, this is how we will start…"

Chapter Twenty-Two
The First Day

Uri sniffed the air. Forest smells were not familiar to him. He sensed a sweet, tangy fragrance, especially when they tramped through those long green needles that fell from the tall feathery trees. The damp odor of moss crept through everything. His feet padded along on layers of forest litter. No one could hear them...only their smell could give away their presence.

They had been traveling for three hours, and had been through the area of scattered trees. They now were deep into the forest. Ahead the path broke into several small trails, leading in different directions. Uri was glad Oden came along as he pointed in an easterly direction without thinking twice.

Within a few yards down the path, the wind began and dark clouds filled the sky.

"Do you think it will rain?" asked Jai.

Goth looked around. "It might. Even though the rainy season is a few weeks away, we could still get a small storm."

As they trudged through the forest the humidity became weighty, and the blowing wind made it difficult to make their way up the hilly road that lay in front of them. It seemed to Uri they had been walking down this path all afternoon.

"How far are we from the river?" Uri had to yell in order for Oden to hear him.

"About two hours. It might be wise to set up camp and wait out the storm."

Uri was glad they all agreed to find a sheltering place among the trees. They began to set up a camp. Soon all of them snuggled around a fire and watched the wind assault the foliage. The trees swayed, the bushes seemed to tremble, and dead leaves swirled in concentric mounds. They prepared a simple meal and silently ate. As sun began to set, the rain came. First slowly, then picking up until the noise from the pelting drops made conversation difficult.

One by one, the men hunkered down in their sleeping gear, protected by a large tarp. The wind died down, and only the patter of rain sang throughout the darkened forest. Uri knew everyone was awake, but heard no conversations. Each one of them was lost in their own thoughts of what lay ahead the next day.

***

Luwanna huddled under her blanket. She looked down on the group from her perch high in the trees. The tree she carefully chose was a sturdy one, with strong branches that couldn't be tossed around by the wind. It took her longer to climb than she thought it would. Her arm was causing some trouble, but ever determined, Luwanna moved up into the tree where she was safe. She didn't need a fire to keep the animals away, and could see everything below. The darkness kept her hiding place from prying eyes, but one expected the rain, and it wasn't pleasant by any means.

Why she had followed them, she couldn't say for sure. Not only did Luwanna have the desire, but also the belief they would have a need for her. It went against all logic. Five fine, strong young men, why would they need her? Luwanna knew she was fearless, and wiry. She could creep into places no one else could. She was fast, and could go into a place and out again, like a ghost. Surely, there was a reason she came. What it could be, she had no idea, but there would come a time when she would find out. Luwanna was sure of it.

Her arm ached. She had used it a lot today and it tended to hurt whenever the weather was damp. She pulled out some leaves and chewed them. Perhaps she would come across a piutti tree that the leaves came from, and replenish her supply.

The arm had almost been useless for many months after the attack. Faithfully, Luwanna kept massaging and moving it. Then she held objects as she exercised it. It was terribly painful, but she was determined to continue. After a year, she managed to have almost ordinary usage of it. She even began swinging on trees, but walking on her hands, as she used to do, was beyond what she could handle.

If only she could stop the nightmares. The grotesque image of the getiru was always on the surface, ready to lunge into her consciousness. She shivered, brushing away the ugly thoughts. Luwanna watched the men curl up in small heaps while she methodically broke apart a biscuit. The wind had stopped and the quiet of the forest made her drowsy. She put away the food and closed her eyes, nestling against the padding of the leafy branches. Morning would come much too soon.

***

Uri turned over in his sleeping garb. He opened his eyes to a dim world of smoke and damp odors. He looked at the fire someone had made earlier. It was a comforting sight, and he enjoyed the smoky odor that hovered over the area. He also detected damp moss and soil. This type of world was so foreign to his senses that it caused him to be very wary of his surroundings.

He looked at Coran and Oden squatting by the fire with steam coming from cups held in their hands. Uri's stomach gurgled.

Lying on his back, he snapped his fingers in their direction. "Biscuits and eggs, please." A sandal flew past his ear. "Well, at least pour me some of whatever you are drinking."

"Get up and get your own." Coran laughed. "Are you going to stay in bed till noon?"

"Noon...the sun is just rising" Uri replied. "Hey Jai, why aren't you up?"

"Too wet." A voice came from beneath the covers.

Slowly, one by one, all emerged from their warm sleeping rolls. They all stood, sipping on the hot crost. They shared a blessing over the biscuits, and devoured them.

"We should be reaching the river soon. It will be tough going and slippery, so we will have to move slowly." Oden said. "If you are all ready, follow me."

They picked up a trail leading into the heaviest part of the forest. The trees made a canopy above them. Strange calls and grunts filtered down along with the growing sunlight. Uri kept looking up to see what animals were making the noises. When he did that, he would stumble over tree roots. It did not take long for him to learn to look where he was going.

"We are entering the Bast area now." Oden said. "I am sure they already know we are here."

"That's great." Jai said. "There goes the element of surprise."

"Who said anything about surprise?" Oden answered. "We need to be clever, and go where they don't think we will.

However, the way we must go to sneak up on them is more dangerous. They won't be surprised, but hopefully caught off guard."

As they traveled on, Uri was seeing trees and plants that were strange and foreign. He also thought he saw one of those keymons through the trees once.

Soon they could hear running water. "I hear the river." Oden whispered. "We must be very close."

They crept along, and then Oden put up his hand. "We need to rest here."

"Where, exactly, is here?" Goth asked.

Oden picked up a stick and drawing a line in the dirt he said, "We have come down this path. We stopped here over night." He made an "x" in the middle of the line. "Then we followed this path. The river is over here." He made a squiggly mark next to the line for the path. "The Bast village is way over here. After we get across the river we take another path this way." He drew to the left.

"How do we get across the river?" Uri asked.

"That, my friend, is the question of the day." Oden smiled grimly. "There is no bridge."

"How do the Bast get across? They bring furniture and bags of goods when they come to the Marketplace." Goth said. "They must have a strong ramp somewhere."

"When they are finished with their bridge or ramp, they destroy it, or at least take it apart and hide the pieces." Oden looked up from his map. "We need to find things they use or build our own."

"Oh great." Jai sighed.

A sudden thrashing noise came from the forest, close by. As they all looked in the direction of the noise, an ugly black animal was headed their way at great speed.

Chapter Twenty-Three
The Attack

It came at them, seemingly from nowhere, and was upon them in an instant. No one had time to grab a weapon, knife, or spear. It hit Oden first, but he was already on the ground and gave a great kick with both feet causing the animal to tumble over his head. The beast was all black with large paws and long claws protruding from them. It was bigger than a getiru and uglier, if possible, with red glowing eyes and long, yellow fangs. The whole face seemed wet and frothy. In an instant, the animal was on its feet and prepared to attack again. Goth was closest and he got it full force. The animal bared its fangs, and saliva drooled from its curled, snarling mouth. An utterly unholy shriek emitted from the animal.

Oden had has knife unsheathed by now, so did Coran. As the animal dug into Goth, the two men jumped on its back and plunged their bone knives into it. They stabbed at it, repeatedly.

It felt as if time stood still. Why wouldn't it die? Uri joined in, with a spear that lay next to him. Blood poured over all of them, the animal's and Goth's mingled together in a horrifying red wave of wet, sticky fluid. The shriek came again. The animal shuddered, and slumped on top of Goth.

They pulled the animal off and tried to assess the damage. Coran soaked a cloth with water and wiped Goth's face. No injuries there, but his arms and left leg showed both bite and claw marks.

It happened so fast. One minute they were standing around, just fine, the next minute, chaos, and blood everywhere.

Oden and Coran began cleaning the blood off Goth so they could assess the wounds. Uri saw Jai standing away from the group shivering. He went up to his friend.

"He's going to be okay."

"Oh yeah, what do you know that I don't." Jai said, his voice shaking.

"I'm trying to be positive, that's all." Uri patted Jai on the shoulder. He got a fresh wet cloth and gave it to Jai to wash off the spattered blood on his arms.

"Thanks, sorry…" Jai wiped his arms, and then put a hand over his mouth. He tried to hold the sobs in.

Finally, Coran had made his assessment of the damage done to Goth. He stood and looked at the rest of them. "It looks like he has surface wounds to his arms, but the wound in his leg is very deep. He must get back to the village."

"I'll take him." Jai straightened up.

"I must go with you. He needs to be carried." Coran pursed his lips together. "It is very unfortunate. Only two of you will be left to fulfill our quest."

"We can do it." Uri spoke boldly.

"I will get back as fast as I can." Coran said.

They constructed a type of sling from forest materials. In the front, it wrapped around the carrier's chest so his hands would be free. In the back two poles emerged from the sling. A person could grab the poles and carry it.

Coran prayed before they left. It went deep into the souls of the four surrounding Goth, as he went in and out of consciousness, moaning, and rolling his eyes.

It scared Jai. "He's going to die, I know it... Lyshon was right."

"Jai!" Uri raised his voice to him. "Listen to me. He is only in shock. He will be fine. You have Coran to help get him home. By then, Goth will be yelling at you to give him a less bumpy ride."

Jai cracked a smile.

"Be calm and trust in The Creator."

"Yes, you're right."

Uri and Oden waved at the three as they left, headed back the way they came. Uri's palms were sweating. What was their mission? At first, it was to find Zekod. Then the need to find the antidote took over. Now the mission was just to stay alive. A shiver of fear ran down his back.

***

Luwanna was quite a way back, and could barely hear what was happening. However, she kept them in sight. She traveled close to the ground in the brush. Then she saw them stop and saw Oden drawing on the ground with a stick.

Suddenly there was a black thing flying around the men. It must be an animal. She heard screams and shouts, then a terrible howl that caused her to cover her ears. The scene in front of her eyes was indescribable. Luwanna tried to look away, but it was if she had no control of her eyes. All her world fastened on the sight directly in front of her. She saw blood

135

flying everywhere, then the flash of knives and spears. Finally, it was over and the horrible animal fell dead.

Who was hurt? "My Lord," she prayed. "Let everyone be safe, especially Uri."

She crawled closer to get a clearer view, and saw that Goth was hurt. Observing the sling they made, she knew he was going back. As Luwanna watched, Coran and Jai carried Goth back to the trail they had come from. She seemed to know he would be all right, but that left only Uri and Oden to carry out the mission. Now they needed her even more.

***

Uri took a deep breath. The incident left him shaken, and unsure as to what the outcome of the mission would be. With only himself and Oden, the task ahead seemed overwhelming. The importance of finding Zekod faded into the background. Without Coran, Uri did not want to get involved in a battle with Zekod, or anyone hiding him. The Dombara people needed help to combat the poison in their bodies, so finding the antidote took precedent.

Looking around, Uri saw nothing but high trees, large looming plants, and a tangled mass of roots on the ground. Vines hung like long, green fingers, some reaching to the ground, wrapping, and winding around the roots as if they were trying to pull the giant monsters up by their toes.

A few faint streams of light traveled through the dense foliage, thinly touching the ground. Uri could hear the buzzing of insects invading a patch of nearby grass, and birdcalls drifting down from the tall tree branches.

He turned his attention to the bloodied black beast they had just killed. Uri felt his stomach quiver.

"We need to move the animal under the bushes over there." Oden pointed to the left where the clearing ended and brush mingled with trunks of huge trees.

Uri did not want to touch it. "Why can't it just stay where it fell?"

"When the butcher birds find it, they will let everything in this forest know that something died. We don't want that known. It might alert the Bast and they could come to investigate."

"Do you know what this animal is called?" Uri asked.

"It is an ebor, and very rare. I am sorry we had to kill it, but they are extremely aggressive."

Uri wasn't sorry. Between the getiru, and this ebor, he surely didn't enjoy the wildlife on the continent. In the land of the Pinolas, he only dealt with the wona, lizards, and other insects. The only hints of dangerous animals were the stories of a howling monster in the North Country, but that was only a myth.

Oden moved beside the ebor. "The hoperls will find it first and devour it within hours. There are so many of those little varmints, they'll take care of the carcass for us."

"What do hoperls look like?" Uri's knowledge of animals in this land was increasing rapidly.

"They are five or six inches long, hairless, with long skinny tails, long thin noses, and large pointed ears. Their skin is brown, and they live in openings between the tangled roots in the ground eating everything, alive or dead, plants, or animals."

Together they each picked up a large, claw-filled paw and dragged it to the brush. They strained and pulled, grunting at the heavy sagging animal. Uri could hardly stand the stench

137

that wafted up to him. "Do they always smell so bad?" he groaned.

"Yes." Oden said.

When they finished, Uri washed his hands with some of his drinking water. "What a nasty task that was."

"I know, but it had to be done. Let's hurry and get to the river before it gets much later."

They picked up their bedrolls, making sure their knives were handy and water pouches strapped to their wrists.

Chapter Twenty-Four
The River

Uri followed in the wake of Oden's trail through the brush. Moving quickly, his companion seemed to know exactly where to go. Soon they were standing on the edge of a gulch that looked down into the Bast River. The water ran swift and rough over rocks, and into several fiendish eddies. To fall would be the end of life for man or beast. From where they stood, the sound was thunderous. A mist circled up and wet Uri's face. He felt like stone, not able to move as he watched the turmoil below. How could anyone cross that? Yet the Bast did, all the time. What was their secret?

"I can read your mind." Oden smiled at Uri's troubled face. "Yes, it can be crossed. They have equipment to do just that."

"Where is it?"

"We have to find it...or, find another way. Let's walk down the bank for a while."

Uri followed, staying a good measure away from the edge. He looked up into the trees and down on the ground, filled with leaves and vines.

"Vines!" Uri took a vine in his hands. "Maybe we could make a bridge across with these."

"How?" Oden looked at the green stringy vine.

Uri cut a long piece from one and gave Oden the other end. "Pull... pull as hard as you can."

The vine consisted of fibers and when they applied tension, the fibers tightened and grew stronger. It felt sinewy in their hands, and became taut.

"How much weight can it take?" Oden wondered.

"It seems to grow stronger the harder we pull on it."

"Well, I want to make sure before we get halfway across and it breaks." Oden grabbed another one and tossed it up and over a high branch. He tied it together and sat on it like a swing. Bouncing up and down, he grinned at Uri. He stood up and they examined the vine where they tied it together. Amazingly, the knot had fused and they couldn't find the seam.

"This is great. I wonder if the Bast know about this." Oden whispered.

"Okay, this will work, but how do we construct a bridge from it?"

Oden squatted and put his hand up to his face, stroking it. "Get me several pieces of wood, hefty and about a foot long."

Uri nodded, and began looking. Strewn under the large trees were many branches and wood. Uri watched from the corner of his eye, in case any more animals roamed around.

"How is this?" He brought Oden a couple long, thick branches.

Oden tried to crack them, finding they were thick, and strong. "These are good. Find more like this." He wrapped the vines around and through the bundle, tying them with knots. He pulled at the knots until they disappeared. Oden made several of these with very long vines, putting the knotted bundles at both ends.

"Are you thinking what I am?" Uri asked.

"I don't know. What are you thinking?"

"We throw them across and hook them on logs or something, then secure them at this end and go across." Uri suggested.

"Go across...how?"

"Hand over hand." Uri answered Oden timidly.

"Correct. Are you up to it?" Oden asked.

Uri knew he was strong enough and agile enough, but was he brave enough? He didn't answer Oden. The stocky, young man began walking along the edge of the gorge, looking at the opposite side for something they could use for an anchor. Uri followed, dragging the vine contraption they had made.

"Look over there." Oden pointed down from where they stood. "There are lots of logs and brush. I think that would anchor the wood we wrapped the vines around."

On the opposite side of the river gorge, lay several downed logs of various sizes, and brush growing among them, creating a place that could hook and hold quite a bit of weight... or so it looked. They ran to the spot, and Oden looped the vines around his arm and with a mighty toss, he threw them across the gorge.

"Ugh, not far enough." He pulled the vines back up to him. It fell into the gorge, heavier than he expected. Oden surged forward. Uri held his breath, but Oden kept a firm grip on the vine. "I'm Okay." He reassured Uri.

Together they pulled it back up from the depths of the gorge and over to where they stood. Again, Oden swung the vines with the wood around his head, and then hurled it across. This time it went further, and hooked behind the mass of logs. They pulled hard, sat on their haunches, and pulled back, again. Then Oden secured it on their side around a tree and they repeated the pulling exercise.

"Looks good." Oden said. "You realize we only have one chance at this. If it breaks loose, we're gone."

"I think we should go one at a time." Uri suggested. "If one of us gets across we can make sure it stays tight so the other one can cross safely."

"I have another idea." Oden said. He ran and grabbed another long vine, wrapped it around a high branch several times, and tugged on it with his whole weight.

"Tie this around your waist. If you fall this will be a safety backup. "You go first. If the vine bridge fails, I will be here to help you get back up to the ground. You weigh less anyway."

"That's true." Uri nodded and swallowed hard. Why was he so afraid? He knew the Lord was directing their paths and would protect them. However, the anxiety grew the further they traveled.

Uri gulped down the fear. It tasted like bile. He tied the safety vine around his waist, watching as the knot melted into the vine. It was strong, and if he should fall, it would hold his weight easily.

Praying, he grabbed the vines with both hands, and when he was off the ground, he wrapped both legs around them. Slowly he crept; hand over hand, over the raging river below. Uri couldn't breathe. He moved along, one inch at a time. It seemed as though hours passed. He didn't dare look down, but he could hear the river, and feel the spray from it. He almost felt frozen midway, but he managed to put one hand in front of the other, and keep on going. What else could he do? About midway, they both heard a snap. Frozen, he dared not move, but the vines were as tight as before. Uri began again, this time as fast as he dared.

Reaching the other side, he motioned for Oden. "Come on, it's okay."

Oden came across at record speed. Now safely on the other side of the river, they adjusted their packs and moved with caution down the path in front of them, leaving their vine bridge behind.

Chapter Twenty-Five
Luwanna's Discovery

Sitting high in a tree, Luwanna watched as Uri and Oden struggled with making a vine rope bridge. She sat comfortably, between branches with her feet up and her back against the leaves. She came down when they began to look for a place to throw the vines. She moved in silence, following in the brush, careful not to seen.

Luwanna had hoped they could find the Bast's bridge to cross the river. It was not to be, so as she watched Uri and Oden construct the vine contraption, she thought how clever and brave Uri was. She hadn't made her mind up about Oden, and remembered seeing him around in the village he seemed aloof, and a bit snobbish. She only knew he was half Dombara, and half Mudan. She also heard he spent many years as a child in the Bast village.

Now she had to figure a way to use the vine rope bridge they constructed. If her left arm were normal, she would have no trouble crossing. She had to think of a way to cross without the use of one arm, and she had to do it in a hurry. They would leave her behind quickly.

When the guys were out of sight, she emerged from her hiding spot. "Let's see," she mumbled aloud, "maybe a sling under my arms." Working at top speed, she constructed a three-way rope, crossing the vines at the center to make a Y.

Then she added one to wrap the vines around. It looked something like a harness. Then she wrapped a vine around the vine rope bridge. She put her arms in it and sat on the edge of the cliff. If she pulled on the front vine, it moved her along the bridge. Not very efficiently, but it would get her across, and she only needed one arm to make it work

"Now, I hope it doesn't break." Taking a deep breath, she began her slow trek across the river.

The roar from the river below caused her heart to pound so hard she could see her chest move. She was almost across when she looked down. In the mist, she thought she could see rock formations protruding from the sides of the gorge. However, the glance down left her shaky and unable to breathe. She thought of the safety rope. In her haste, she forgot all about it.

Suddenly one of her sandals fell from her foot. Instinctively, she reached for it, and yanked hard on the vine wrapped around the rope-bridge. She watched her sandal tumble in rapid descent. The mist was so thick she couldn't see it hit the river. Once again, Luwanna began to edge closer to the bank and safety.

Then it happened. The vine rope was shredding from rubbing against the rope bridge, and the yank when she lost her sandal, tore it. As it slipped toward the edge of the cliff and safety, it snapped. Luwanna didn't even realize she was falling until hitting a ledge that protruded from the side of the cliff.

It was not a long fall, but it hurt as she landed on her back. Stunned she laid still for a moment. "Well…thank you my Creator." She prayed. Sitting up she looked not at the river below, but a hole in the side of the bank. Getting on her hands and knees, carefully so not to fall off the edge, Luwanna crawled to the large hole. Roots and small rocks protruded from the opening, but it was the only way. She couldn't climb back up and she definitely was not going down. Therefore, clearing the opening, she crawled with apprehension, into the hole. As she entered, it opened up inside and was larger than it appeared.

The only thing that bothered her was the darkness. As she moved further in, away from the opening, it was so dark she could not see her hands as they moved in front of her. She prayed this led to the top of the ground, and not to a dead end, trapping her with nowhere to go.

Luwanna realized that when she came out, she would have to figure out where she was, and which way the Bast village was located. As she contemplated the dilemma, the hole turned upwards and she could see light. Then she saw them, hundreds of slimy creatures. Her hands were full of those tiny, white things, and slimy mud. Gagging she hurried to the opening, and out onto the cool, dry ground.

She rubbed her body on the ground ridding herself of those disgusting, wiggly things. In some places, they had begun to suck blood. Luwanna grabbed large handfuls of leaves, wiping her face and neck. Pulling herself to a tree, she leaned back and shuddered. Trying to calm down she took deep breaths.

A few minutes later, she was able to look around at her surroundings. The sun was getting low in the afternoon sky. She figured the sun was in the west, so she needed to travel south. Standing on shaky legs, she began to head in that direction, hoping to find some clues to direct her to the Bast Village without them capturing her.

She traveled off the trails, moving slowly in the brambles. She endured the scratches because it was safer. The roots from the tangleroot trees began to grow in great, heaving coils. Catching a foot among them would be easy. She noticed an occasional hole, like the one that contained those foul white, slimy creatures. They were a place to hide, if necessary, but the thought of crawling back into a hole made her shudder.

As the sun was setting, she smelled the faint odor of smoke. Where was Uri? He had to be close by. It was time to climb a tree once again. Luwanna needed a very tall one. She was good at climbing so the fact she had to climb high didn't faze her. Finding the right one was tricky. It was getting dark quickly now. She hunted for the right tree, and finding one to her liking, she began to climb. Her left arm ached terribly, but she had to continue, no matter how painful it got, and she was now out of the leaves of the piutti tree.

Up she went, higher and higher. It took skill and patience. She had to decide which way to go. The trees were crooked, and branched off in many angles. When she reached the height of one branch, and saw another going even higher, she climbed back down to it, and traveled a different path.

Up, always up. Luwanna never looked down. She looked at the surroundings in front of her, and above. She found herself in a good spot. She knew Uri and Oden would not make a fire, so it would be harder to spot them, but whose fire did she smell? In the growing darkness, her eyes scanned the area slowly.

She thought she spied them a couple of times, only to realize it was just the bushes moving.

She finally looked down, and to her surprise, they had bedded down almost directly below her. If she rustled the tree or made any noise, it was certain they would hear her.

As she watched them eat a simple meal of biscuits and dried meat, her stomach made hideous noises. She was thirsty and hungry, but did not dare do anything until they were asleep.

Luwanna heard them decide to travel further when it was late and dark. It would be long into the night, so in order to get some rest before the dangerous trip, they went to sleep right away. She slowly removed her pack and dug quietly into the depths for her water jug, and stash of food. Not bringing enough, Luwanna had to ration the food. She hadn't eaten all day, except for some berries she stumbled across before she got to the river. Now, a whole biscuit went down quickly. It barely quieted her hunger, but that was a good thing. It helped to keep her awake through the night. She planned to follow them into the village in order to be handy if they needed her.

The thought of capture worried her, so she passed the time by thinking of different scenarios, and tried to plan a way to rescue them. Luwanna believed she would be a surprise. The Bast might know the men were here in their territory, but not about her. At least she didn't believe they did.

Chapter Twenty-Six
Time for Disclosure

Uri lay very still on his sleeping pad, and watched the first moon begin to rise. He knew that both moons soon would be in the high in the sky. He and Oden would have to deal with a night flooded with moon glow when they set out for the village. Fear rose again in his chest as he thought of capture. What would the Bast do to them? Maybe they would give him to Zekod to do whatever that evil man liked. That was a real nightmare, and he trembled. He began to sweat, even though it was very cool. Why was he so afraid? He had been fighting fear from the beginning, and it was winning.

The spirit of fear was not from The Creator, he knew that. However, none of his emotions were under control now. The anger he felt for that painted boy, or the faint distrust of Oden, would not go away. The desire for Coran almost consumed him, and fear of an animal rushing at them in the middle of the night kept his nerves raw.

Uri would be no good when the time came to enter the village and search for the antidote. Oden continued in his secretive manner, and remained closed-mouthed about it. Not having an exact plan wasn't Uri's way of doing things. He thought about not following Oden and staying behind. It was comforting to play around with the thought, but it also was cowardly. This time he had to rely on The Creator for his very life. He had to know deep in his soul, he was doing His will and whatever happened, The Creator would protect him.

He looked up high onto the tall trees above him; the branches criss-crossed into a maze.

As his eyes traveled up, up in the very tops, he chuckled. His imagination was working overtime. He thought he could make out a figure of a girl huddled down among the branches. He began looking for other shapes that looked like objects. Then Uri thought of Luwanna. He was glad she didn't come with them. She was safe in the village with her family and friends around her. Not out here in this cold, rainy forest with wild animals and danger everywhere. Yes, Luwanna was safe and he wanted it kept that way. He closed his eyes and dozed off.

***

When Uri opened his eyes, Oden was moving about, preparing to break camp. Now what was he planning? It was time for Uri to demand firmly for more information. Where they were going, what they were going to do, and what the plan was. Uri was too frightened to continue heading into the unknown. He sat up and without moving further, watched Oden.

"Aren't you going to pack up?" Oden asked.

"No."

"What's the matter?"

"I'm not going anywhere until you reveal everything to me." Uri stated.

Oden smiled. Uri knew Oden was enjoying this game. He knew everything, and Uri knew nothing.

"I want to know your plans, in detail." Uri waited.

"I think it is time. I didn't want you to know everything in case the Bast captured you. I thought it was best you were kept in the dark as long as necessary."

"Does Coran know where we're going?"

"Yes." Oden sat back down across from Uri. "We have a contact among the Bast people. He has helped us many times. He helped us get the antidote for your tribe. He has told us that Zekod is among the Bast, and has maneuvered his way into the confidences of many leaders, especially the unsavory ones."

"But Zekod isn't the main focal point anymore, right?"

"No, the antidote for the Cheekee fruit poison is. However, we need to contact my friend first. He will help us find a supply of it."

"Do you know what the antidote is?" Uri asked.

"Yes, I do, and so does he. The Bast guard everything heavily, so we need his help. Even then, it is still dangerous, and there is a high chance we may be captured."

Uri fidgeted, the knot in his stomach tightened, and a desire to go home dominated his mind.

"Who is this friend?" he asked.

"His name is Bo. When I lived with the Bast, we became good friends. Our beliefs and dreams seemed to be as one. After I came home, we stayed in touch. Have you ever heard the call of the butcherbirds? It is very loud and distinct. That was our signal to meet at the edge of the river. We varied it from the real call, but the Bast people would never know the difference."

Uri felt that old fear began to rise in his throat again. "What will happen to us if we get caught?"

151

Oden's brow furrowed. "I really don't know. Not with Zekod in the picture."

They continued to pack up, and Oden moved onto a trail. Uri followed behind. He wished Coran would return in time to help.

***

It was about midnight when Coran and Jai entered the Dombara village carrying Goth. The watchman sounded the alarm, and immediately the leaders of the village met them. Ando reached the litter first, and noticed it was his son.

Coran spoke up. "Goth will be all right. It is a flesh wound from an animal, but he needs it to be cleaned and attended to."

They went to Ajaben's home. Jai and Coran released Goth into his capable hands then continued to Jai's house. Lyshon was there. The word Goth was brought back injured spread quickly, and she was preparing to go to him.

"I knew he would get hurt." she said with tears in her eyes.

"He will be fine." Jai reassured her.

Her eyes glared at them both. Without a word, she ran out the door.

"She'll get over it." Jai sighed.

"I am leaving immediately to go back and find Oden and Uri. First, I need food and water to replenish my supplies." Coran waved as he turned, and ran down the steps.

After filling his pack at his own house, Coran stopped at the home of Elajon and Marga to check on Bibbi and Sarella.

Elajon met him at the door. "Is Goth alright? I heard the alarm."

"Goth was injured by an animal. Jai and I brought him back. He will be fine. Oden and Uri are alone, so I need to get back quickly. I wanted to see how the children are doing."

"No change." Elajon said.

"I must leave now."

"I understand, and will offer prayers to our Creator. Uri and Oden need you." Elajon held onto Coran's hand. "Please be careful."

Coran nodded and headed out into the night. He followed the trail he had come from. By himself, he could make good time, and would be back at the river in a couple hours, maybe less.

When he reached the place of the attack, Coran noticed the body of the animal was gone. He continued to the edge of the river, and looked up and down. He squinted into the darkness. Somewhere Oden and Uri had to create a way to cross the river. He began to walk to his left. He thought he saw a rope crossing the river, so he inched closer; sure enough. He touched the handmade vine rope bridge.

"Very clever, but how did they construct it?" He said to himself. *"If it held them, it should hold me."* Then he spied the safety rope lying near the edge of the cliff.

"What are these things made from? It looks like vines." He examined the safety rope, and tugged on it. He jumped up and hung on it with his whole weight.

Finally, he tied the safety rope around his waist, and hung on the vine rope bridge. Giving up his safety to The Creator and the vines, Coran crossed; hand over hand, with his legs wrapped around in front. As he crawled to solid ground, he noticed a frayed rope hanging from the bridge. It was disquieting. Hanging alone, without telling a tale of how it got that way, or if someone dropped from it.

He didn't have time to investigate. Coran continued down the dark trail.

Chapter Twenty-Seven
Regret

Kee left the village late in the afternoon. He looked for a place where he could think. Since he attacked the two Dombaras, a vague uneasiness slowly consumed him. It was a mean thing to do. The girl was so scared, and the fact he actually cut her appalled him. Hunting and finding animals was one thing, but hunting humans was entirely different.

When Master Tau told him what he needed to accomplish for his forehead paintings, he didn't think it would matter what or who he hunted. Kee looked forward to the stealthy adventure. He snuck into the Dombara village with his heart pounding, and the excitement of hunting the boy down was fun, a great challenge. However, once he completed his task, he felt sick about it. This surprised Kee. Face painting was very important to him, but he wondered if his older brother Bo would agree. Bo didn't see eye to eye with the leaders of the village, or his father. He even moved out of their home into his own place.

Kee sat in a thicket of bushes and looked at the ground, trying to calm the voice inside his head, and make some sense of his feelings. He sat for a long time. The first moon rose slowly over the treetops with a weak light. As he thought of his brother, Kee hoped talking to him might help. He picked himself up from the ground, and took a deep breath before heading in the direction of Bo's dwelling.

Kee inhaled the strong, musky odors the forest breathed out at night. He was mystified as to why Bo decided to leave the village, and live in the forest, away from the tribe, the family, and the customs. All the things he grew up with. Bo claimed an area about a mile from the Bast village, and cleared the land himself. He also constructed the hut himself. It was sturdy, made from mud, forest vegetation, and covered with porgour, the gooey matter made from the Dengu leaves. When it dried, it was waterproof. Bo had hinted to him about another secret usage, but no matter how Kee begged, his brother would not tell the secret.

When Kee reached the edge of the clearing, before he could see into it, he stretched up high into some bushes beside him. He felt for the hard surface of a bell. It made more of a clacking sound than a bong, but enough to let Bo become aware of company. Only family and closest friends knew of this device.

The bell wasn't the only device Bo had constructed. He also took vines, and stripped them into several long pieces. He then tied them together making a long rope. He strung the rope around the area, and surrounded his hut. No one could enter without setting off an alarm, not a noisy one, but one he recognized as an invasion of his property. Kee thought his brother was one of the cleverest Bast in the whole village, and smiled at the thought of Bo relaxing in the chair he made from the surrounding brush and branches. Hanging it from a low branch in the tree next to his hut, he loved sitting and swinging in it.

Kee pulled on the bell and watched Bo come to the gate. His brother had wide set blue eyes, tall, and had a pleasant face that smiled easily. He put his hand on Kee's chest, and said an amazing thing. "How is your heart?"

Kee closed his eyes. He always felt peaceful in his brother's presence. "Not very good."

156

"Come in and we will talk about it." Bo opened the gate. It shut behind them. They walked the several feet to where Bo had built his hut. Kee perched on the front step. Bo sat back down in his seat and reached up to clasp his pet guanat, a small, dark, nocturnal animal. With its elongated forelimbs and fingers that supported a thin wing membrane, the creature crept down his arm and settled on Bo's hand, waiting to be petted. Bo's face showed worry, and concern. "I heard about the task given to you, finding a Dombara boy named Uri, and threatening him."

"I hurt the girl that was with that boy I was sent after." Kee confessed.

"You did what?" Bo's eyebrows closed into his forehead. Kee knew Bo was very upset when his eyebrows took on that appearance.

Kee tried to explain. "I was told to bring back the boy's blood on a cloth, but I thought it would be stronger magic to bring hers."

"I have told you, there is no magic. The healer Tau is not a good man. Listen to me. You must be careful what you do."

"I want to be like you. You have all the body paintings. You have been very brave."

"I don't believe that way anymore. I got the paintings only to please our parents. I never attended the meetings."

Kee stood up. "I know. I miss you, and think you are wrong."

"I will explain many things to you some day. Now, sit down and tell me about what you had to do."

Kee's face was downcast, and the darkness around his eyes told of a deep unhappiness.

Bo spoke again when Kee was silent. "I thought these body paintings were very important to you."

"I thought so too, but I didn't like what I had to do in order to receive that last one."

"Tell me exactly what Tau told you to do."

Kee squirmed and looked away from Bo. "You know of Zekod, the Pinola man our tribe has taken in. I don't like him. He is changing the way our men think. Even with our sometimes-brutal rituals, he is adding evil. He bullies everyone around, and forces his convictions on the leaders."

"Yes, I have had a couple run-ins with him." Bo placed the guanat back on the tree. The small animal climbed to a branch, and hung upside down by its tiny feet. With large round, black eyes, it watched Bo intently.

Kee sighed. "From what I understand Zekod is wanted in his land for a murder caused by using our poisons. Uri and his cousin are here to find him, and bring him to justice. I was sent to frighten them away." Kee rubbed at his face, agitated. "I had to find the boy Uri and catch him. Then warn him to stay away. Last of all, Master Tau wanted me to cut him, and put his blood on a cloth embroidered with the figure of the Spirit Chun. I wanted to please the master, and when I actually had the boy in my clutches, I grew mean and hateful. Instead of cutting him, I cut the girl that was with him. I cut her on the throat."

"You did what? You cut an innocent girl?" Bo was clearly horrified.

"I only poked her, so I could get some blood on the cloth. I thought female blood was more powerful. As I traveled home, I felt sick to my stomach. I wondered if I was becoming like Zekod, and that thought has haunted me ever since."

Bo stood up and covered his face with his hands. He sighed and told Kee, "It is one thing to desire to please Master Tau, but that is not our way. This has happened because of the influence of Zekod. He has brought great evil into this tribe. Master Tau had never sent anyone out to injure a person before. I know there are many rituals and secrets. We are suspicious of other tribes, possessive of our herbs, medicine, and the wood that grows in our territories. Some men even feel superior to the other tribes in the land, but never has the Bast hurt others intentionally."

"Do you think this pleased the Spirit Chun? In our house we honor him with an alter and fresh flowers. I only want to please the Spirit." Kee blinked away the tears forming in his eyes.

Bo came over and sat next to Kee. "I don't believe in the spirits anymore. They are a superstition. I have heard of a better way."

Kee gasped. "Really, you don't believe in the Spirit Chun, the Spirit of health and happiness?"

"No."

"What about the Spirits Tok and Saf?" Kee asked.

"No, none of them, those are spirits we have invented."

"Oh." Kee looked at the ground. "What do you believe in?"

Bo was several years older, the eldest of five children. Kee was the youngest. He had two other brothers, but his whole life he hung on to Bo, proud of his brother's handsome face, and strong frame. Kee hoped to be like Bo some day. He admired his brother's convictions, determination to believe his way, and not allow the tribe's ideas to influence him.

Bo began to rustle the bushes around him. He looked to see if anyone was in the vicinity before he continued to talk.

His vision was more than excellent, and his intuition above average.

"I don't like Zekod either." Bo spoke softly. "In fact, I hope the Dombaras do find him. He did some very evil things to his own people. He is loud and arrogant. He thinks he is the boss of everyone in this tribe. It makes me furious that the elders let him strut around, and tell everyone what to do."

"What did he do to his people?" Kee asked.

"Zekod did not like the new beliefs growing among his people. He believed this new way caused him to lose profit from the old superstitions. His control on the elders and others were slipping from his hands, so he and his sons tried to frighten the new Believers, and ended up killing one of them. The tribe went after him, and some of his companions that were with him. He fled and came here. Because some people in our tribe had helped him obtain the poisons, they felt compelled to protect him. However, I think there is more to it than that. He has something to offer. I don't know what, yet. If the tribe wants to protect Zekod, there had to be a strong reason."

"Yes, but what is this new belief Zekod is so afraid of?" Kee became very curious.

Bo stood up suddenly and put his finger to his lips. "Shh…"

Chapter Twenty-Eight
Visitors

Kee heard a distinct rattling. Someone was approaching, and not in a friendly way. Bo went in the hut and came out with a long spear.

"What's the matter?" Kee whispered.

Two shadowy figures advanced to the gate. The tall one threw it open and, as the moonlight fell on his face. Bo recognized the red mark, Zekod. The other stayed in the darkness.

"What do you want here?" Bo's voice was threatening.

"The village knows your friends are in our territory. I've come to warn you." Zekod said.

"My friends in *your* territory; since when has the Bast village become *your* territory?" Bo advanced, tightening his grip on the spear.

"That don't matter. You've been instructed not to meet with 'em, or do anything to help 'em."

"So, why are they here?" Bo asked.

"Some people in the Pinola tribe have been poisoned by the cheekee fruit. They believe it is the Bast's fault" Zekod grinned.

"Is it?"

"Don't help 'em in any way." Zekod warned, ignoring Bo's question.

"Or what?" Bo walked up to Zekod. "I don't take orders from you or anyone else. Will you poison me too? Remember, you are a foreigner here. You might hold sway over some of the men, but do not push your luck."

They glared at each other. Zekod blinked first.

"I'm here to give ya a friendly warning."

"There is nothing friendly about you." Bo spit out.

Kee looked into the shadows, trying to figure out who the second intruder was.

Zekod turned his attention to Kee, frozen in fear. "Tell me, young man, did ya enjoy your adventure with Uri? I hope you cut him good!" Zekod laughed, then turned and the two left the way they came.

Kee turned to look at Bo. "You have friends among the Dombaras?"

"Yes, I do. If their people have been poisoned, as Zekod says, my friends will be here soon to see me."

Kee rolled his eyes in disbelief. "Oh, now what?"

"You, my brother, will have to decide whose side you are on, Zekod's or mine. My friends could be here at any time."

"What does that mean? I am Bast and so are you. That doesn't mean the Dombaras are our enemies."

"No," Bo said looking to the spot where the two visitors disappeared, "but Zekod is."

Uri marched behind Oden. The thought of them heading towards disaster, plagued his mind. The ground had a different smell to it, dry and dusty. The trees grew thicker and brambles hindered their progress. It was slow going, however soon the area cleared and Uri saw a hut, encircled by a fence of some kind. Oden shook the fence and a rattling noise emitted from it.

Outside, close to the hut, smoke from an earlier fire trickled up into the surrounding trees. It was just a wisp, and Uri could tell who ever lived here had retired for the night a few hours ago.

In a flash a man appeared holding a weapon, Uri could make out the shape of a short spear.

Oden spoke out in a strange language.

The man dropped the weapon. "Can't you come to the front?" He laughed and grabbed Oden's hand.

It was a strange sort of handshake. Uri realized it must be a special sign between the two. The man lifted up the fence and Oden went under. Uri began to follow when from the hut emerged a boy about his age. There were no black marks on his arms, but Uri knew without a doubt who it was, and it stopped him in his tracks.

Their eyes connected, and the face of the boy changed. Uri saw terror. That look stopped him from attacking the boy as he had attacked Coran in Marga's kitchen. At that time, he saw the face of a man who harmed his sister, even though it was an accident. Now Uri saw the face of someone who had harmed Luwanna. His arms, legs, and heart wanted to tear into this person, but something held him back. The look on this boy's face was startling.

The boy flung himself at Uri's feet. "Please!" he cried, "I sorry, don't hurt me; very sorry."

By the tone of the voice, Uri would have never known it was the same person. The voice he remembered was arrogant, unfeeling. This boy was afraid and regretful. Uri didn't move.

Bo lifted his brother off the ground and spoke to Oden in a strange language. Oden turned to face Uri. "The boy's name is Kee. He has had a change of heart and begs your forgiveness."

Uri took a deep breath. Of course, he would forgive him. That was the command of The Creator, to forgive all wrong against you, either by friend or foe. However, Uri wasn't ready to let this Bast off the hook, not yet.

"Tell me your name." Uri told him gruffly.

"Kee, I...I Kee."

"You injured someone dear to me. Did you enjoy that?"

Kee looked at Uri confused.

"I know you did." Uri continued. "You had control of the situation. You enjoyed that feeling."

Kee dropped his head low.

"Do you realize what you did was wrong? It doesn't matter why you did it, or who told you to do it. If it is wrong, it is wrong. Hurting people is wrong. Do you understand?"

Kee began to speak in that language again.

"Please," Bo began. "He was told to do that by one of our leaders. This man is under the influence of Zekod. Kee followed a ritual, used by the Bast for eons, to show his bravery as he enters manhood. It has been always carried out

164

with animals. Now it is being distorted. It is not the desire of the Bast tribe to injure other humans."

Bo continued. "Now this man Zekod has infiltrated his own twisted beliefs into our tribe. He has an agenda of hate and evil. Kee was a victim of that." Bo put his arm around Kee, and lifted him from the ground. "He is a good person. He has come to understand that he was used."

Uri nodded. "Yes, I forgive you Kee. Sometimes we have to do bad things to understand the difference between right and wrong."

Kee grabbed Uri's hand. "I thank you. Can we be…friends?"

"Maybe." Uri said hesitating. "We will get to know each other first."

They filed into the hut.

"Tell me… what is going on?" Bo asked.

"The Cheekee fruit your people sold at the marketplace had been poisoned." Oden began to tell the story of how several Dombaras were suffering from the same coma as the animals the Bast captured. "We are here to find an antidote and bring it back to save their lives. But, we must hurry."

Uri looked suspiciously at some food Bo handed him.

"It's dried meat. Kee brings me food from the village every week. It is dried meat from the chola, a lizard. Very good."

"Um…" Uri placed it on his knee. "Tell me, how did you discover this antidote?"

Oden smiled, "When I was living here, our house was near the animal pens. The area, where the tribe kept the ones captured with the poison, was within my view. Outside two women sat grinding large seeds used for making bread. One of them had a small child with her, and wasn't paying any attention to her. The women were chatting, as women do."

Uri grinned to himself at the obvious way Oden thought about women.

"The little girl strayed away and crawled under the fence. Near the shelves by the fence sat a bucket of porgour paste, a waterproofing material. Porgour paste contains Dengu leaves. The child toddled over to it and put her fingers into the bucket. I was amused watching her."

Oden moved, and looked into the sky as he told the tale. "She smeared it on her face. Then she did a remarkable thing. She went over to one of the outnu, laying in a coma. She spread just a little bit on the outnu's nose and mouth, and suddenly it sat up, a bit wobbly, and soon it… just trotted off. I looked around to see if anyone saw what transpired. There wasn't a person in sight, only the two women engrossed in the village gossip. The little girl, startled by the animal, crawled to the edge of the fence, and began to cry. By then the animal had left the pen, and not a single person had seen what had happened. Later I tested that on another animal with the same result. I never told a soul, except for Bo. We kept it our secret."

"Now it can be used to help the infected people in our tribe." Uri said with excitement.

"Yes." Oden said. "However, we have to get it first."

"Can't Kee go and get it for us?" Uri asked. That seemed simple enough.

"Yes, however, alone he would have to wait until he could do it without being seen, and that could take some time." Oden explained. "We need to get it now…today."

"Yes, and I would like to find Zekod, and get hold of him." Uri's face darkened.

"Now that will be difficult." Oden hesitated, and then he turned to Bo. "Zekod needs to be brought back to Pinola Land to pay for his crimes."

Bo shook his head. "I doubt if the tribe will let him go so easily. He has made quite a lot of friends, and also there is that Dombara with him."

Uri perked up. "What Dombara?"

"He arrived here a couple of years ago. Immediately he set about making friends with several of the young men. They formed a kind of group, influencing the leaders in many ways. They were into some kind of trading deal, very hush-hush."

A cold, ominous trepidation enveloped Uri. What did this mean? Something bothersome nagged at his brain. The Dombara he saw at the ancient ruins reminded him of someone. Who? Oden interrupted his thoughts.

"Well, how shall we go about getting the porgour?"

"If we all go to the village now, while it is still early," Bo said. "The pens will be deserted. Kee can divert the attention of anyone that is hanging around."

Uri looked to the horizon, and the faint promise of a new day. *"How will this day end?"* He thought to himself. It could go either way. One thing was sure; they would either be on their way home, or…

"We'll go around to the back area, it is against the woods." Bo drew on the ground. "After we get inside the pen, it's a short walk to the shelves and cupboards."

"We won't need much. A small container will do." Oden added. "Like this." He reached over, and picked up a small, squatty clay jar with a cover from under the hammock.

"That would be perfect." Bo nodded "Now, after one of us fills the jar, we come back here." he looked at Uri. "I know you want to get hold of Zekod, but I honestly don't know how."

Uri shook his head. "Never mind that. As much as I would like to pound the saving grace of our Creator into his thick, ugly head, and drag him back to Pinola Land, I have no desire to go after him by myself."

Chapter Twenty-Nine
Captured

They reached the village before the sun totally rose. In the fading darkness, they all peered through the fence and looked at the rows of unconscious animals, and the area of the shelves and cupboards.

Kee had gone another way, around to the front by the entrance. He would be the lookout for anyone coming.

"Uri." Oden whispered, "Squeeze through the fence and get the jar filled, quickly."

Uri's stomach did the flipping act again. He located the area. It was several feet away. He could traverse it in a few seconds, but his feet turned to heavy, unmovable stumps.

"Go!" Oden's voice trembled.

Spurred on by Oden, Uri began to move, through the fence, and toward the bucket of porgour. Every movement was in slow motion. He approached the shelves, and on the lowest one sat the special bucket.

Uri peered into the dark abyss of the storage compartments and reached with his left hand to fill the jar. At that moment, Oden hollered, "Run!" but before he could move all went dark. Someone tied something around his head. He realized he had a blindfold over his eyes, and now captured.

Uri, not being able to see, listened intently to the noises around him. Scuffling sounds told him they had captured another of his group. Rough hands shoved them inside an enclosure. Uri sat where his back was up against cold wooden bars. He heard someone speak that language he didn't understand, and Uri recognized the voice of Kee speaking back. Two men were yelling at Kee. They punctuated their voices with obvious sounds of slapping, and shoving.

Uri felt closed in, and had the impression he was inside a cage not large, or very high. He felt Kee's body fall onto his. In an instant, the blindfold was gone and he blinked, trying to adjust to the brighter light. He was in a six by six foot cage, about three feet high. The bottom of the cage also was made of wood, and he saw only one opening locked with a large bolt. Kee lay on his side against Uri's legs. Red marks, from the slaps, made a criss-cross mosaic across his face and back.

"What happened?" Uri whispered.

Kee looked at Uri. "They caught us."

"I know that, but what went wrong?"

"Someone got suspicious. When they saw me... around the front. I think Oden and Bo got away." Kee whispered. "I hope they rescue us, soon."

Uri felt someone jump and land on the top of the cage they were in. He looked up to a shadow made by a human form. The face came down closer to where Uri could see his features. He recognized them immediately, and his breath caught in his throat. "Rill."

"Hi there little buddy. Surprised?"

"I...I thought..."

170

"Yah, you thought I drowned. Not me… not old Rill. I just floated along till I landed here." He gestured around. Grinning and touching his lower lip with his tongue. "In the land of plenty; plenty of food, plenty of drink, and plenty of power."

"What are you doing…?"

"Here?" Rill finished the sentence. "Living as I please." His face darkened and his eyes closed until they were slits on his face. "You left me to drown."

"No, I looked and called for you. I passed out, and found myself on a sand bar."

"Sure, after you thought I was drowned. It was your fault my mother died."

"Your mother died the day we were abducted." Uri tried to explain, but Rill was in his own world.

"I hate you more than I did then." Rill jumped down and opened the bolt that locked the cage. He pulled both of them out, one at a time, and tied their hands in front of them, "I would kill you now, if I could. But someone wants to meet with you." He sneered at Uri cryptically, and shoved them both around to the dark area by the forest.

Uri noticed how Rill had changed. He cut his hair in the Bast style, his clothing, completely Bast. He attempted to meld into the society. However, there was one thing that gave him away. Rill could not change his orange eyes to blue.

His face was still wide and full. Now it looked a little older, and a cruel light glistened in his eyes. He had not grown any taller, so now Uri could look down on him, even if it was only a few inches.

While Uri stood staring at him, Rill pushed him hard into the waiting arms of Zekod. The twisted mouth looked fierce, and his red mark glowed like harsh flames on his face. Rill grabbed Uri's arm.

"Well, hello, are you lookin' fer me?" The grin turned upside down. "Here I am." He spread his arms wide.

Uri went numb, he thought about the grand words he wanted to tell Zekod, about the grace and love of The Creator, but they fell into dust at his feet as he stared at the sight of the evil standing in front of him.

"I'm not as squeamish about killing you as Rill is." He started forward and Uri knew Zekod was going to kill him with bare hands. Uri needed time, and talking to this lunatic might buy some.

"Wait," Uri called out in desperation. "Don't you want to know what happened to your wife and sons?"

Uri would never be able to tell him. Zekod's eyes widened and began to bulge from their sockets, as unbelief and horror flickered in them. His mouth opened and blood trickled from one corner. His jaw slackened and the trickle turned into a red surge, covering his chin and staining his clothing. A gurgle emitted from him, as life fled from his eyes. He fell forward towards Uri, landing on his face in the dirt and gravel. A large knife protruded from his back.

Rill bolted, as if all the pagan gods in the world were after him, disappearing into the forest. Uri looked up from Zekod's body to the gleaming eyes behind the knife.

"I had to." Oden said calmly. "He would have killed you. I count it an honor to take his life."

All the commotion brought out the people in the village, and in seconds, dozens surrounded them. The leaders of the tribe pushed through the crowd, and looked at the dead body of Zekod.

Uri knew they were in big trouble. Oden stood very close to Uri. However, Bo was nowhere in sight.

"Who did this?" The Master Tau asked.

Oden spoke up. "I did. Zekod was about to take the life of my friend. It was in defense of Uri that I killed him."

They looked at Uri. "Who you?" They spoke in their pidgin tongue.

"I am a Dombara. I came to find Zekod, and take him back to Pinola Land where our elders can question him in the murder of a Pinola woman. He poisoned her."

There wasn't any doubt among the leaders who took Zekod's side. They stood together and scowled in unison. "Why you kill him?" one asked.

"I didn't." Uri said. "He was about to kill me."

"I see no weapon in his hand." The one in front, examining the body spoke.

"He was about to do it with his bare hands." Oden voiced.

"Yes, ask Rill, if you can find him." Uri pointed to the forest where he vanished.

"You come with me now. You, Oden, and Kee too." The men who were Zekod's allies pushed, and hustled them to another pen. This one was much larger.

"You all stay here. We talk."

Kee pleaded, "Master Tau," and spoke again that strange language. However, it did no good. The Bast men turned, and left them in the pen with the early sunshine filtering down on them.

Chapter Thirty
Discovery

Luwanna forged ahead. She came across Bo's hut surrounded by the fence. However, by the time she arrived there, everyone was gone. She saw Uri and Oden's packs, which told her they had been there.

She paused only for seconds, then followed the path that lead into the Bast village. It didn't take long before she knew the village was near. Keeping to the bushes and off the path, she heard voices rise and fall. She slowed down, and then stopped.

Luwanna looked around. There had to be a tall tree nearby so she could climb to the top. She would be able to see into the village, and view what was happening. She ventured further in the forest away from the path. Finding one in the center of a grove of tall trees, she began to climb. It was slow going, not only because of her arm, but she had to choose which way to go up the tree to reach the top safely.

When she finally arrived, the view was spectacular. Not only was she able to look down on the area where the Bast held Uri, Oden, and another boy, but into the large area where the animals were laid out, side by side. They obviously were in that 'coma state'. She needed to find the antidote. Listening, she hoped they might reveal something that would give her an idea of where to look.

The day light grew brighter as she sat up high. Around Luwanna were many trees, almost as tall, but she had her back to one that was especially close. She intensely focused her attention at the group of people questioning Uri, so she heard or saw nothing else.

A rustling sound came from behind her. Before she had time to turn, words reached her, close to her ears.

"Well, well, well, Kerka."

Luwanna shocked to hear a voice, and a familiar voice at that. Turning to look across the branches, she stared into a face she hated and feared.

"Rill." His name came out of her like a squeaky whisper.

As Rill took time to bask in the glory of discovering and surprising her, Luwanna half scampered, half fell down the tree. She ran into the bushes, never looking back to see if he was following. Tearing through the brush, she knew exactly what to look for. She noticed a couple more openings in the ground coming over to the village. They were just like the one she traveled through to get away from the river, and she knew what lay inside.

Even so, Luwanna ran straight to one, and fell on her hands and knees, crawling into the opening. She ignored the mud and slime, and she didn't care if those creatures crawled over her. Pulling the brush over the hole, she dug deeper with her fingers. She closed her eyes, and didn't dare to breath. Those things began to crawl on her. Luwanna felt them on her arms legs and all over her face.

Someone made a lot of noise, heaving through the brush, but never came close to where she was hiding. Keeping her eyes closed, she waiting what seemed a long time. She finally emerged from the hole covered with mud, slime, and worms.

They covered her face, arms, and legs. Anywhere bare skin was available. She quickly rubbed herself with leaves from any brush she could reach. Luwanna rolled in the brush, frantic to rid her body of those nasty, slimy creatures, and continued to wipe everywhere with leaves. Finally, Luwanna lay back against the tree, shuddering. She looked at the many bleeding areas that the worms had attached themselves, and sucked out her blood. Even though it was a gruesome experience, Luwanna felt good. She did it. She escaped from Rill. Now she could help Uri and the others.

***

Coran found his way to Bo's hut. It was bright and sunny by now, as the morning grew old. He entered through the gate and looked around to see if anyone was about. He noticed Uri's and Oden's packs lying near the doorway. The silence was deafening. Coran knew something or someone nearby caused the strange quiet. He slowly turned full circle, studying the ground, structures, and brush. His hand tightened around the spear he brought back with him.

"Over here." Clearly, it was Bo's voice, and it came from the bushes surrounding the front of the property.

Coran sighed. "What is happening?"

Bo came into view. By the look on his face, Coran knew things had gone wrong.

"We tried to get the porgour, but Kee and Uri were captured. Oden and I got away, so he stayed there to watch, and try to rescue them. I came back to get some weapons."

"Do you have a plan?" asked Coran.

"Not really. We need to go back to see what is transpiring."

As Coran and Bo left to return, Bo filled him in on all that went on, including the introduction of Kee to Uri. "The boy has changed his ways and now I believe he will not be able to stay in the village."

"First we must finish what we came here to do," Coran said. "Then we can deal with Kee."

Chapter Thirty-One
Sentencing

Uri sat erect in the cage, watching the deliberations of the elders going on in front of him. Examining his emotions over the last hour or so, Uri realized the fear and terror he had been experiencing all this time, was now gone. He faced the worst and survived. Now he understood the power of The Creator, and how faith could carry him through the "fire." Nothing would undermine this faith again. It felt good to be free of the nagging debilitation that fear brought. The peace and contentment of faith filled every part of his body, soul, and spirit.

Uri looked over at Kee, and wondered what he believed in. In this culture, as in the Pinola's, belief in Spirits ruled their lives. Oden had told him how the Bast turned their Spirits into gods, with names and powers. The more characteristics and powers the gods received, the harder it was to dislodge the beliefs. If Kee believed strongly in the god Chun, it would be hard to give up the faith he placed in this false deity. Faith in something familiar was comforting.

The men talked in their own language, loud and obviously disagreeing. Uri leaned over to

Kee, "What are they talking about?"

"They argue what to do with me." Kee struggled with Uri's language. "Tau wants me released to him. Zekod's friends want... punish me. The others want me to go live with Bo."

"Who do you think will win?" Uri asked.

"Tau win, you watch."

After much talk, and gesturing, two Bast men came over to the cage. One was Master Tau, the other a man who looked lovingly at Kee. Uri knew that was Bo and Kee's father.

The father opened the cage, and beckoned them to come forward. "Kee, you will go with Master Tau. You will be his apprentice and live with him."

Kee looked up, and bravely spoke back. "No, I will not go with Tau. I will go and live with Bo."

Tau began speaking to Kee in the Bast language. When he finished, Kee shook his head.

"I do not belong to you. No one has the right to sell a person to another."

The father glared down at Kee and Uri. His blue eyes grew dark and menacing. "I am your father and I give you to Master Tau. If I receive a gratuity, it is none of your business."

"I do not recognize your right to give me away." Kee's resolve held strong. He stood straight, with his head up, glaring back at his father.

Again, they spoke loudly and with much anger in their language. Kee looked sideways at Uri. "They are going to imprison us."

"Young man," Master Tau addressed Uri. "You guilty in the death of Zekod, and we hold you here until we agree on punishment. Kee, you also stay here until you come to your senses."

During the furious argument with Kee, Uri saw from the corner of his eye Oden slip out of the open cage, and disappear into the brush.

The leaders marched Uri and Kee over to a small building with only one door, and window. A large piece of wood covered the window, so no one could see in or out. They walked inside, and Uri looked around. On the floor lay two mats for sleeping, and an area to sit with a table. As he walked through the room, he noticed the back led outdoors into a pen. He wondered if the Bast used this building for animals.

"You both will stay here. Someone will bring you something to eat in a few minutes. Water is provided outside, in the pen." Kee's father looked long and hard at his son. Then he walked out the door, shutting it behind him, and left them alone.

Uri laid down on one of the mats. "Now what?" he said to himself.

Kee hearing him replied, "Bo and Oden will come for us."

Uri rubbed his eyes. "I know they will try."

Food came and they devoured it. Again, Kee and Uri were alone. From looking beyond the pen in the back of the holding house, Uri saw two Bast men approach. They wore a headdress, and had their arms and faces painted with black markings.

"Oh…" whispered Kee. " The protectors of the gods."

"What does that mean?" Uri asked.

"They are either coming for me, or for you."

The men marched around to the front of the house, and opened the door. A command barked out in Kee's language.

"They told us to come out." Kee interpreted.

Uri and Kee went out into the filtered sunlight, and stood in front of the intimidating men.

"You," one pointed to Uri. "Come with us. You come to give homage to the god Chun."

"No." Uri spoke up without thinking twice. The other man looked at Uri and spoke quietly. "We give you chance to be free. You come and ask Chun to forgive you. It is a privilege and an honor to have our god forgive you."

Kee leaned over and whispered in Uri's ear. "Go, you don't have to believe. They want to give you a chance to be released."

Uri took a deep breath. He wanted to be released. He wanted to go home. But, he knew this was something he could not do.

"No." He said again.

The men half carried, half-dragged Uri across the ground, through the village, to the front of the temple. There they threw him to the ground at the feet of Master Tau. In his robes, and headdress he looked intimidating. He glared at Uri, his eyes squinting with scorn.

"You bow to our god Chun."

"What will you do if I don't?" Uri asked.

"You die."

Chapter Thirty-Two
Courage

The spirit god, carved from a single rock, produced awe in everyone who gazed upon it. When you looked at it from one side, it was silver and shimmering, from another direction it became coppery. As beautiful as the stone was, the beast it depicted was grotesque. It had a body of a man, with a long, snake like tail. Its giant arms rested on huge columns, and the long, sinewy fingers ended in great claws. However, the face was what made Uri shudder. It had a fierce animal face with lips drawn back, exposing sharp teeth and a beak-like nose with gleaming eyes all across the top, Uri counted six. Each eye held a dazzling red stone.

The head appeared to grow long, wormy ropes. It was twice as tall as an average man was. Behind the idol were six four legged beasts, similar to the getiru. Three were on one side, and three on the other. They looked wooden with a polished, golden glow, like the tangleroot.

Everyone was silent. Uri looked around, and noticed Kee stood close to his left. The Bast tribe had surrounded them from behind. They came out to see what this Dombara boy would do. It was a simple thing, just bow, and then continue to go about your business. Go home, back to the forest, free.

No one in the village expected Uri to believe, or claim this god as his own. It was a control mechanism, nothing more.

However, it was something Uri could not do. No matter what happened to him, he could not, would not, turn his back on The Creator. Even the act of bowing was an affront to the holiness of The Creator of the Universe. This "thing", this idol disgusted him.

Uri looked directly at Master Tau. "I will not bow to anything on this world. It did not create me, or you. You have created it." Heavy silence followed. "I do not intend to insult any of you, or your beliefs. However, you should not force your beliefs on me."

Uri bowed his head, looked at the ground, and prepared himself for swift action, his death, torture, or something just as horrible.

"Go back to the house." Tau pointed. "Out of my sight."

The rough hands grabbed Uri and Kee. In a moment, they found themselves back in the holding house, and alone.

***

As Bo and Coran walked down the path to the village, Oden emerged from the side, through the brush. "They have been taken to the holding house." he whispered.

"Can we get them out from there?" Coran asked. He was afraid for Uri, knowing Zekod would do something to him. "Can Zekod hurt him?"

"We don't have to worry about Zekod anymore." Oden nodded his head. "He is getting his reward as we speak."

Coran took a deep breath. He understood what Oden meant. "What about the two other men that left Pinola Land with Zekod?"

"No other men reached the Bast village with him." Bo said. "When he arrived in the boat he was alone."

Coran took another breath. What an evil man Zekod was. What wicked crimes had he committed? Now, it was all in The Creator's hands. Justice manifested itself in many forms.

"Well," Coran spoke again. "What can we do?"

"I'm not sure. It is guarded. Even when everyone goes back to their homes at mid-day for a meal, the guards will stay." Bo said.

"How many guards did they place at the holding house?" Coran asked.

"Only two." Oden added. "We should be able to overtake them."

"We still need to get the porgour." Coran reminded them.

"It should be quiet on the streets about now." Bo said. "Let's approach the animal pens, and see if anyone is moving about."

They bent low, and moved with careful silence. Bo slid under the rails of the pens. Within seconds, he had a jar full of the precious goo. Almost crawling, he came back out, and they hurried to the concealment of the bushes.

"That was almost too easy." Coran breathed once again. "But where are the boys?"

"Past the animal pens, and over to the left of the cages." Oden looked at the porgour.

"Coran, you should leave with the antidote now, and get back to the sick in our village."

Before the three men could say any more, someone laughed, loud and coarse.

As they turned to look, the laughter stopped. Rill stood at the rails of the pens.

"Don't bother to run. I see you in the bushes. If any of you move I will scream for help, and dozens of Bast will be here in seconds."

"What do you want, Rill?" Coran asked.

Rill grinned and walked over to the men. "Why do you think I want something?"

"If all you have to do is yell, why haven't you done that?" Oden said. "What do you want from us?"

Rill's eyes narrowed and his face pulled together in the middle, causing his mouth to pout, and his eyebrows to meld into one single line across his face. "I want two young women. I don't care where you get them. Bring them to me where the sea meets the land beyond the village. Bring them in the middle of the night." His mouth twisted cruelly, "And I want Uri too."

"I know why you want Uri, but why young women?" Coran was mystified.

"I need to pay a debt. That's all you need to know."

At that moment, something fell from a tree landing on Rill. Without thinking, all three men rushed him. To everyone's shock and surprise. Luwanna stood up with Rill's arm bent hard on his back.

"Here," she said to the men. "You take care of him. I'm getting Uri." She flung Rill into Coran's arms and fled across the village to the holding house. No one was in sight.

"Uh…" Bo asked, "Who was that?"

"A friend of Uri's." Coran said, and then he turned to Oden and Bo. "How did she get here?"

"Your guess is as good as mine." Oden answered, and then ran after Luwanna.

185

"I think we should tie up Rill and take him to your place." Coran said to Bo. He stood behind Rill, holding both hands in his, while Bo stood in front, stunned at what just took place.

Rill twisted his hands hard, freeing them, and punched Bo in the face, knocking him to the ground. Then he spun around, and kicked at Coran. He connected his foot in Coran's stomach. Coran doubled up in pain, and Rill was gone, disappearing into the forest.

"Coran," Bo groaned. "Don't bother with Rill. Go back and take the porgour with you. Go quickly, before anyone sees you."

"But…" Coran protested.

"No, you must go while you can. You need to save those children and others in your village. We will rescue Uri, do not fear."

Coran knew he was right, and he began to run towards the forest and the river. To get home with the bowl of porgour was the only thing that made sense. That was why they came. Now he fled, and as rapidly as possible. He would be home in a matter of a few hours.

***

Uri and Kee sat facing each other on the rickety chairs with their hands tied behind them. Kee looked bleakly out the back, and Uri saw the unspoken fear as it consumed him.

"In your opinion, what will your people do to you?" Uri asked.

"I will be sent to live with Master Tau. I will belong to him, like a slave. If I run away and they catch me, I will be considered an undesirable, and be put to death."

"What is an undesirable?"

186

A sad film covered Kee's eyes as he looked at Uri. "Any Bast who does not behave honorably, who will not conform to the beliefs, does not worship the gods, and who disobeys the Master. He or she is an undesirable."

"Bo does not conform to their beliefs, and he is not arrested. The tribe leaves him alone." Uri pointed out.

"He was never given to Master Tau. The tribe considers my situation an honor. If I disgrace that honor, I am an undesirable, because I have brought shame to the whole tribe."

"What do you think they will do with me?"

"Oh, you will die."

Uri swallowed hard, and his heart leapt to his throat. He stared at the floorboards under his feet. Battered and broken, they told lonely, sad stories of many people brought here over the decades. People who didn't uphold the Bast standard waited punishment with trembling and dread.

"We are just two more in a long line of prisoners". Uri thought.*" Many more will come behind us. But... we are different. I am a follower of The Way. Surely, the Savior will not abandon me. He didn't when I was on the sand bar. Why would he bring me this far just to...?"*

"No, they will be here to rescue us." He told Kee with confidence. "Don't be afraid. The Creator loves us and will not allow evil to triumph."

"I don't understand what this Creator is, but I have figured out, all the gods of my people represent evil." Tears spilled from his eyes. "It is very hard to accept, and it hurts."

Uri realized that for generations, pagan beliefs controlled the life of the Bast people. It would take a lot of time and

187

incredible effort to break through, and gain a foothold to bring the Truth to them.

Uri was about to reply when from the corner of his eye he caught something moving. In a flash, the warm body at his ear spoke in a whisper.

Chapter Thirty-Three
Liberation

"Shh… I am untying your hands." He knew the soft voice of Luwanna.

In seconds, he was free. As Uri untied Kee's hands, the Bast boy's eyes locked with Luwanna's. She gasped as her hand flew to her throat.

"Relax" Uri whispered. "It's ok now…go quickly."

Luwanna motioned to them to follow her. "I came in from the back." She said. Behind the house, in the pen, they saw a hole.

"Climb in this hole behind me. It's a tight fit so you will need to wiggle through it. Keep your eyes and mouth closed, but follow me and we will come out over by the trees."

Uri and Kee followed a dirty and ragged looking Luwanna into the blackness of the hole. Uri felt as if he would smother, but once committed, he moved forward. Even though he followed Luwanna's instructions and kept everything closed tight, his eyes were full of grit and his mouth tasted dirty. However, in a few more wiggles he would be free and on the ground.

As he emerged, looking around, he looked at his companions and they looked at him. Suddenly, Uri and Kee yelped, frantically wiping their faces and arms. Uri decided to roll on the ground. Luwanna had failed to mention the worms and slime.

"Quiet." Luwanna cautioned.

Uri used his shirt to wipe the dirt from his eyes and slime from his face. Kee also shuddered from the amount of crawling things he wiped from his body.

Uri spoke up, "What are these things? How horrible. Did you know these were in this hole?"

"Yes," Luwanna held back a chuckle. "I have encountered them a couple of times, but they make these holes so we can't be too critical, can we?"

"Look," Kee whispered. "They enjoy the taste of your blood."

"Do you know about these repulsive creatures?" Uri asked Kee.

"Yes." Kee shrugged his shoulders. "They are slopboers, and have given us the means to freedom."

The three were in the safety of the forest, and far away from the eyes of anyone near the holding house. Kee and Luwanna were right. It did not matter what was in the hole. They were free.

Uri grabbed Luwanna by the arm. He couldn't believe his eyes. "Where did you come from?" Uri stammered. "You are supposed to be home where it is safe."

Luwanna put her hands on her hips. "Are you sorry I came?"

Kee looked from Uri to Luwanna and back again.

"I can't say that I am." Uri answered." Did you follow us from the start?"

"Actually I left before you did. I stayed in the tops of the trees and watched you most of the time. I saw the attack of the black beast, watched Coran and Jai as they started to take Goth back. I even went into someone's home and found your packs. I was in a tree watching as they captured you. Then Rill found me. I got away and I outsmarted him. Those holes in the ground come in handy."

"When did you first come across them?"

"I'll tell you all about it later. Let's get out of here first."

Uri took the hint and shut up. Then it hit him, Rill tried to get his hands on her. He felt fire shoot from his eyes. Not as long as he was alive would he let Rill hurt her.

To his left, he saw two heads just above the bushes. He realized those heads belonged to Oden and Bo. How could he attract their attention without attracting the Bast? Then Luwanna flew past him, her legs bent and close to the ground. Within seconds, he saw their heads turn toward him and following in Luwanna's direction, they sank down to the ground.

Kee pointed at them. "They come to help us?"

"Yes." answered Uri. "They are here to help us."

One by one, they formed a line and crept out of the village area, heading toward the river.

***

Uri sat near the cliffs of the river gorge. When they arrived, and were all gathered, Oden turned on Luwanna. Uri knew he was eagerly waiting for a proper time to question her extensively.

"Young lady, why did you follow us?"

Luwanna turned and faced Oden directly. "I decided to follow so I could assist you when it became necessary."

"What made you believe you, a girl, and one with a bad arm at that, could help us?"

"You do not know me." She lifted her chin.

"How did you manage to come all this way without us seeing you?"

"I hid in the trees. I am a good climber, one arm or two, it makes no difference."

"Did you realize you could have put all of us in extreme danger?" Oden scolded.

"I was the one to stop Rill so Coran could leave with the porgour, and I rescued Uri and Kee. Earlier I escaped Rill by outsmarting him. I outsmarted you too." Luwanna smiled. "I crossed the river by altering your vines… because I only have one good arm." She struggled not to be sarcastic.

"Well, Oden, she is right on every count." Uri said.

"Yes," Oden was loathed to admit.

"Now, aren't you glad I came along?" Luwanna tilted her head, looked at Oden, and batted her long eyelashes.

Oden smirked, as he looked away.

Uri wrapped up the questioning. "Luwanna, do you know how crazy you are?"

Finally, all seemed well. The antidote was on its way to the village, and everyone was alive and safe. Bo would be able to go back to his hut and live in peace. No one would be able to prove he had anything to do with the death of Zekod, or the intrusion of the Dombaras, namely Uri, Oden, and Coran. The only problem was Kee.

He would have to leave the Bast area in order to stay alive. However, he voiced how he wanted to stay with Bo.

"If you stay with Bo," Oden pointed out. "They will arrest him also. You will be putting him in danger."

Tears of frustration fell on Kee's face. "I have nowhere to go. I refuse to be Tau's slave. I can't stay with Bo. What will become of me? I am Bast, and this is my home. I no longer trust in our gods, but I don't understand yours." He nodded to Uri and Oden.

"Maybe I should no longer live." He bowed his head as the tears left his face, and spotted the ground.

Bo knelt beside Kee and covered him with his arms. "Don't talk like that. We all have crossroads in our lives. This is one of yours."

Uri sat down in front of him. "None of this was an accident. You attacked Luwanna and me. Then your brother helps us. These acts are no coincidence. I am sure it seems very confusing at the moment, but there is a design in all of it."

"What do you mean, design?" Kee wiped his face with his sleeve.

"You said you don't understand our God. Let me tell you about Him. He is The Creator of All, everything you see and everything you don't see. He loves and cares for us. He designs our lives."

"Did he create our gods?"

Bo stood up over his brother. "Those are not gods, they are created in the minds of the leaders to control and manipulate the people."

Kee shook his head. "I still don't know what will become of me."

"Let's move on." Oden motioned to move everyone along. "We have to find the Bast's foot bridge across the river. We can figure out what to do with Kee later. It's getting very late."

With Bo leading them through the thickets, they arrived at the spot the Bast hid the bridge. Oden and Bo assembled and dropped it by a rope across the river in record time. They all crossed and left it as they hurriedly traveled up the path.

They left it so Bo would be able to use it to get back across the river, and return to his hut.

Chapter Thirty-Four
An Evil Plan

Rill slipped through the trees and brush, with anger in every footstep. He was infuriated that he had to stumble into his camp without Luwanna. She had too many protectors, but there would come a time she would be alone.

He resurrected thoughts of capturing Luwanna when he accidently stumbled across her in the tree. It would have been the perfect disaster for Uri. If Rill had added her to the group, that would have been the wallop to crush his enemy.

The first thing he saw was Dree, napping on the cloth he had strung between two trees. With all the fury pent up inside, Rill kick the bottom of it, and sent his Bast companion sprawling on the ground.

"You worthless piece of …. I told you to watch the girls."

Dree picked himself from the ground, and stood in front of Rill, looking ashamed. "They are still tied up in the hut." he spoke in his Bast language.

Rill had exhausted his anger, so he shook his head. "We are going to bring them to our friends tonight. It will be a long voyage, so get them ready."

Dree slithered into the hut, while Rill took over the hammock. He closed his eyes. His dream of ruining Uri was beyond his grasp for the present. Zekod had promised him two Pinolas in exchange for the poisons. That never happened.

Earlier Rill had made a deal with his contact, Tri-Po from the Umbinga people, to bring him four young women. Rill was only able to obtain three. He captured those from the mountain people. They weren't the fair women from the Dombaras, or the brown beauties of the Pinolas, but they were healthy and strong. The slender, tall maidens surely would be pleasing to his friend, and supplier of the osis root. However, he still must face those people without one of the promised women.

Rill knew he could talk his way into postponing his promise, and go to the other villages later. Luwanna would always be there, and so would other young women. If he found himself against the wall, he could trap a young Bast girl or two. Maybe he would add an extra one to sweeten the pot. These people always needed young girls and women, and he always knew where to find some.

Dree, however, was becoming a handicap. Dree found him floating off shore in the southern part of the Bast land, half drowned from the storm when he and Uri escaped from Dombara Land. During that storm, Rill managed to hang on to the pieces of the overturned boat after it broke up. Dree pulled him onto the shore, and helped him breathe again. Dree's parents fed him, and kept him warm until he fully recovered from his ordeal.

He had hoped Uri drowned, and it wasn't until he contacted Zekod, and his two boys that he learned Uri had returned to Pinola land. Rill was furious. Uri had left him to drown while he paddled his way back home. It seemed to Rill that his plans never succeeded. He would have to try harder.

Dree was the one that had introduced him to the osis root. Ingested in powdered form, it helped to give your body great strength, and open your eyes to wondrous things. One had to be careful not to use it very often, or you could end up like Dree, with the mind like mush. Rill used it when he needed to expand his mind and body, enjoying the exhilaration it gave.

It seemed to Rill that everyone wanted something. Zekod wanted poison for his purposes. So Rill saw an opportunity to get what he wanted by supplying Zekod with the poisons. Those people to the south wanted women, and they possessed the osis root. Rill wanted the osis root, and had to make promises to get it. However, Zekod did not come through with the women needed to complete that promise. To obtain his supply of osis root he would have to be clever, very clever. These people must continue to trust him.

Drifting into a light sleep, Rill stayed in the hammock until it was time to leave. It would be a long, cold trip and they needed to carry supplies: something warm to sleep on, fuel to make fire with, food, and water. Dree loaded those on the women, and prepared the sleds to pull.

Rill knew the fiendish pleasure Dree took in punishing these women whenever he could. That could only go so far. They had to be strong in order to make the difficult trip, and still be in good shape when handed over. Rill examined every move Dree made, and by the time they left, he was satisfied. They would be able to arrive at the appointed time.

Chapter Thirty-Five
The Mountain People

The night had been cold and very windy. Uri and his four companions had huddled together for warmth, but he doubted if anyone got much sleep. The clouds kept any moonlight from glowing down on them during the night, so it was pitch black for many hours. Uri peeked from his covers at a day dawning sunless and dull. He was glad to see the area they had bedded down, a small, shallow opening in the rubble of boulders that lay at the foot of the western hills.

Uri sat up and rubbed his eyes. There was no smoke from a cheery, morning fire. They couldn't allow a smoke trail to give them away. Not as long as they were in Bast territory. The only good thing about this dreary morning was the thought of home. By tonight, he could be in his bed at Elajon and Marga's.

He began to pack up his equipment like the rest of them were doing. Bo and Kee had shared a cover. They had no time to outfit themselves for a journey. Luwanna walked around stretching. "I prefer sleeping in a tree to sleeping on the ground." she declared loudly.

"What are the plans?" Uri mumbled.

Bo spoke first. "I suggest we travel up into the mountain country instead of pushing through the forest. If anyone is following us, it will stop there. They don't go up there, as a rule."

"Yes," Oden said. "I agree."

"During the long night, I thought of stopping at the mountain people's village. I am on friendly terms with them." Bo explained.

"They prefer to keep to themselves, and don't mingle with the other tribes." Oden spoke up, showing off his education of the area.

"They will be hospitable to us." Bo replied. "I will stay with them for a few days as you travel on."

Uri watched Kee as Bo spoke. He still sat on the ground, his arms wrapped around himself. "Come on Kee, walk next to me, so we can talk."

Kee nodded and a weak smile crossed his face.

The trek up the mountain was easy. The trail was wide and meandered around the large boulders. Uri continued to talk to Kee, with help from Oden, about The Creator and the Savior. Together they began to help Kee understand what the Truth was.

"You tell me we don't have to do things in order for The Creator to love us, and not punish us?" Kee asked, astonished.

"No, our Lord loves you without conditions, sacrifices, or rituals." Bo replied.

"However," Uri pointed out. "You must understand... He sent His only Son into the universe He created to sacrifice Himself for us. Then He raised Him from the grave to return into His realm, and we must believe that."

"Why would He do that?"

"We can't save ourselves. We can do nothing to make ourselves holy or good enough for our Creator. He has to do it for us. It is simple and straightforward. No rituals, just faith."

"However," Oden broke in. "Just faith without following His commands is in vain."

"Faith comes first." Uri snapped back.

"Shh…" Bo whispered and crouched low to the ground.

"What?" Oden whispered back, as the group laid low to the ground.

"Getiru prints, two of them. They're fresh, probably an hour or less in front of us." Bo pointed to them.

"I thought they were solitary animals, and stayed in the forest." Uri asked.

"Sometimes they hunt in pairs." Bo motioned for them to continue on the path. "They follow the outnus up here. Be watchful."

Uri looked at Luwanna and saw how the fear changed her stature. How dangerous his adopted land was, and how safe the Pinola Land actually could be. No wild animals, no savage people, only sand and more sand. However, whenever he went back to go to school he continued to long for the lush green, and diversity of Dombara Land.

It was late morning when they walked into the village of the mountain people. Standing at the edge, the newcomers allowed the village people to become aware of their presence, a polite thing to do. A group of children playing nearby ran to get the chief, and soon he and several of the villagers came over to greet them.

"I am Vakier." The leader stepped forward, and bowed at the waist. "Bo the Bast, good to see you again. I see you have brought others, including a lovely young maiden."

Bo bowed. "An honor to see you Vakier. If you please..." he introduced the rest of the group, leaving Luwanna for last. Uri looked at the tall man in front of them. He wore his hair, like the Dombaras, braided, but Vakier's hair was much darker and streaked with grey. His eyes were the color of the Bast, a deep frosty blue, and they were very round and large. The clothing, also, was much like the Bast. Warm animal skins, not only on their bodies, but wrapped around their feet as well.

The village was laid out in a large circle, with rows of huts extending far past Uri's ability to see. The welcoming party led them to a round hut also covered in skins. Uri wondered what animal lived here that provided such an abundance of material.

It was warm and roomy inside the hut. Everyone sat cross-legged in a circle. A woman, tall as the men, entered and brought them a warm drink. Uri welcomed it, and waited for his body to thaw from the cold and windy weather outside.

Bo spoke first. "We came up here from the Bast village. My companions are Dombaras. They traveled to the Bast area to acquire an antidote for a poison given to many of their villagers. Some of our people did a terrible thing by helping a bad and evil man. My people don't always make good decisions, as you know. I have been helping them escape from the leaders of my village. That is why I brought them up here. They will have to travel through the mountains to reach their village safely."

Vakier nodded along with the men sitting, one to his right, and one to his left.

"You are all welcome to stay here and rest before finishing you travel on to your village. However, there is one sitting next to Bo who is also Bast."

"He is my brother, Kee. He cannot go back home. He has broken a trust made by our father, and will be put to death."

"Your people are hard." Vakier lowered his head. "Where is he to go?"

"We do not know at this time."

The flap at the door opened and a woman, younger than the one before, came in and knelt by Vakier. The women wore their hair in braids like the men, but they adorned it with feathers and beads.

This is my wife, Solera. She has something to tell you."

She stood and bowed at the group. "Someone from the Bast village came here in the dark of night, a week or so ago. Three of our young maidens were taken, against their will."

"You mean kidnapped?" Uri spoke quickly before he thought.

"Yes, in the middle of the night. This has happened before. The legend is the tribe in the south; a lost tribe buys them as slaves. The legend is very old."

"Why are you telling us?" Bo asked.

"It must be someone from your tribe." She answered, looking at Bo directly. "Can you help us find who this is? We want to get our young women back."

Uri felt a cold lump in his stomach and he looked at Luwanna. Her eyes were wide as she met his stare. Is this why Rill was after Luwanna? Was Rill the one Solera spoke about? He was fully capable of such a terrible evil thing. He must be getting something he desperately wanted from the exchange. Luwanna's capture would be a cunning strategic blow against Uri. From now on, he would have to keep a close eye on her.

"When I return home, I will see what I can discover." Bo promised. As Solera left, Uri saw the tears that formed in her blue eyes.

"All we can do is pray to The Creator for their safe keeping." Vakier said.

Uri was astonished. He was not aware the mountain people believed in The Creator also. He was pleased. Kee might be able to stay with these kind people to learn about peace, and more about The Way.

Chapter Thirty-Six
Homeward Bound

The weather began to clear, and pale sunlight splattered around the ground, warming the air. After sharing a meal, they all went outside and circulated among the people. They looked at each other with curiosity.

"I'm cold." Luwanna shivered.

Let's see if we can get a coat made of those skins for you." Uri looked around for Bo.

"Stay here." He ran to Bo, who was standing with Vakier. "Can I borrow one of those skin coats for Luwanna?"

"Yes." offered Vakier. He entered the hut they were standing in front of and reappeared with a coat exactly Luwanna size. "Tell her she may keep it, as a gift from us."

"Thank you." Uri ran back over to Luwanna and helped her put it on.

"Ooh." She exclaimed. "I like the way this feels."

As they walked beyond the huts, Uri began to hear animals bleating. He looked into the clearings, and saw hundreds of bameas.

Luwanna pointed to them, captivated. "Look how beautiful those animals are. The fur, or whatever that is, has a silvery quality, and some are spotted black."

"These are slightly larger than the same animals in the Pinola meadows." Uri noted. "Notice how they seem to be calm and do not attempt to run away. It's as if they know this is a safe place, and that they will be cared for here."

They watched the animals mill about munching on the grass. Uri remembered the group of herdsman with the kavacs he saw on the Pinola meadows on his way down from the hills. The mountain people and the Rabirs kept the same animals. These bameas provided a multitude of resources for both lands. They were the animals providing the skins these people used. He wondered if they knew how to make cloth, as the Rabirs did.

They returned to the center of the village and saw Kee involved playing a game. Uri notice how he seemed to be enjoying himself. Uri believed The Creator lovingly found this place for Kee.

He found Bo and pointed Kee out to him. "Do you think he could find a home here?"

"Hmm… I think I know just the family." Bo grinned. "You see that boy next to Kee, a bit taller?"

"They are all taller than Kee. Everyone here is taller than us." Uri remarked.

"True, but I mean the one…" Bo pointed. "There, he just put his hand on Kee's shoulder."

"Yes, I see him." nodded Uri.

"He is an only child, very rare here. His parents desperately wanted more children."

"But, Kee is not a little child, he is almost grown." Uri pointed out.

"He still needs guidance and love." Bo said. "I think those people would be good for him."

As they walked toward the group, Kee broke away, coming towards them. "Bo, meet my new friend."

Uri felt joy raise in his heart as Kee brought the young man over to Bo.

"This is Pelli."

"I am happy to meet you. I know your parents."

Kee turned to Uri. "This is my friend, Uri. He is very special to me."

Surprised at the comment, Uri could only nod at Pelli.

"Bo," Kee lowered his voice, "Do you think I could stay here with Pelli until the elders in our village change their minds about me?"

"We need to talk to Pelli's parents first. I'm afraid it might be a long time before things change in our village."

"I like it here." Kee pleaded.

"Come; let's go talk to my parents." Pella began to walk toward his home.

"Wait," Bo said. "I will go first and talk to them. All of you stay here." He quickly disappeared among the huts. The boys went back to the game, while Uri and Luwanna strolled over to a bench and sat down. "I worry about your safety. Rill is very dangerous. I wouldn't put it past him to come into our village and capture you." Uri said.

"Hah... I can handle Rill." Luwanna replied.

206

"Maybe not. Think about it, he is obviously involved in the disappearance of those girls, and he was after you. It was only by the grace of our Creator that you got away."

"Well, our Creator will continue to protect me."

Uri shook his head. "I still want you to be ever vigilant. I am going to warn our leaders and Coran too, about Rill."

Luwanna grabbed Uri's hand. "I will be safe, and if it is The Creator's will that I am to be captured, I know there is a greater good in it."

Uri felt his stomach lurch as he thought of Luwanna in Rill's hands. "I'll break his neck if he hurts you!"

"Don't borrow trouble. We are here and I am fine." She replied in a soothing voice.

They looked up to see Bo walking into Vakier's hut with a couple they believed to be Pelli's parents.

Uri and Luwanna waited for them to emerge. Oden came up and stood beside them. His face told a story Uri did not want to hear. Would the request be refused?

Soon they all came from the depths of the hut. Vakier spoke first.

"To let the Bast boy, Kee, stay here is very risky. His people, known for their hostility, are hunting him. His blonde hair stands out. He does not look like one of us. If the Bast were to come looking for him, we would give him up. It has to be that way to protect the rest of the villagers. Even then, they might punish us for hiding him."

Uri's heart sank. What Vakier said was wise and true.

"However, we as a people, and believers in The Creator of All, know it is right to give sanctuary to a young boy who is under a death sentence."

"Thank you Lord," Uri prayed.

Vakier continued. "He will be given a hat to wear whenever he appears outside, and he must keep a low profile."

"Extra guards will be posted in case a patrol of Bast comes this way." Bo added.

Pelli's father stepped forward. "We will be honored to help this boy become a man."

The whole audience cheered. Kee beamed and went to stand beside Pelli.

Oden rubbed his hands together and spoke, practical as always. "Since everything has been settled here, we need to hurry and get ourselves home, before it gets dark."

"The fastest way is to travel north. The trail will lead you to the shoreline of the Green Sea. Follow it until you reach your village." Vakier said.

Pelli's father added, "There is a well used trail that overlooks the sea. Stay on it."

Luwanna, Oden, and Uri packed up, preparing to leave. They said their goodbyes to Bo and Kee, thanked the mountain people for their sacrifice and hospitality, and began the walk home.

Uri's heart was full. Soon he would be with Bibbi and the family. By now, Coran would have reached his village, and administered the antidote to everyone. They would be healing from the poison, and returning to good health once again. The only worry he had left was Luwanna. What was Rill doing now? What were his plans? No good, Uri felt sure of that. Putting one foot in front of the other, they all traveled in silence, lost in their own thoughts.

Chapter Thirty-Seven
The Odyssey Complete

It was getting very late, so Oden wanted to bed down for the night an hour or so from the village. "I want everyone to be awake and available when we arrive."

Uri thought that immodest, and boastful, but he and Luwanna were very tired, so he agreed.

They entered in the early morning and the Dombara people gave the returning three a hero's welcome. They lined the pathways, cheering and whistling. Uri waved at Oden as he went off with the leaders of the village. Luwanna smiled and followed Uri. A few times in the land of the Bast, he thought he would never see the people he loved again; on this side of the sea, or on the other.

"I want to go directly to my home and see how Bibbi and Sarella are faring."

"I want to see your family too." she followed. "Let Oden have all the glory. He will take it anyway."

They entered and the family cheered. "Welcome home, my son." Elajon rushed and hugged Uri tight.

Uri was relieved to see his family again. He learned Coran had gotten back the day before, and immediately set about to treat every single infected person. By evening Bibbi and Sarella were moving about. They even began eating some soup Marga made. "It is good to be home." he said. They went down the hall to where Bibbi and Sarella still shared the bedroom.

"Uri," they cried in unison. He went over and hugged each one.

"Tell us all about your adventure." Bibbi pleaded.

"Soon, but not now." Uri saw Bibbi look at Luwanna so he quickly added. "However, I do want you to know that Luwanna bravely risked her life to help us get the porgour." Uri bent down and whispered loud and clear. "You owe her your life, my little brother."

"You are very brave, Luwanna." Bibbi thanked her.

"I was in the right place at the right time." she answered.

"Was your life in danger, at any time?" Elajon asked as he stood in front of Marga in the doorway.

Uri looked past him at his mother. "I'll fill you in on the details later." He turned and took a deep breath. "Right now, I am hungry!"

"I need to go now." Luwanna took Uri's hand. "My family must be worried sick."

"Okay, stay alert." Uri warned.

Bibbi's head popped up from the pillows. "Alert about what?" he asked.

"That's only for me to know." Uri teased.

Luwanna picked up her new coat. She hugged Sarella and Bibbi, waved at the rest of them, and hurried out the front door.

"I have a feeling terrible things happened to you." Marga twisted her apron in her fingers.

210

"Mother, I'm hungry. Will you fix me breakfast?"

"Oh, of course." She went to get eggs and biscuits going in the kitchen.

Elajon walked Uri to the front room. "Tell me, did you find Zekod? Will he be coming back?"

"Yes, we found him. However, his companions never reached the Bast shores."

"What happened to them?"

"No one knows. No one will ever know. Zekod is dead."

Elajon's eyes opened wide. "How?"

"Oden stabbed him in the back as he was about to kill me."

He slumped into his chair. "The wicked will be punished. If you live by evil and violence, that is how you will die."

"Rill is still alive." Uri continued. "He is after Luwanna. She must be watched and protected."

"Another shocker. Is he...?"

"As rotten as ever?" Uri smirked. "Worse. He and Zekod were behind the poisonings."

"That does not surprise me." Elajon said. "Coran administered the antidote to everyone, but there were a couple of adults that were too sick, and he was too late to save them. I think there were contributing factors to their deaths. One man was sick before he ate the poisoned fruit and another's family didn't take care of him properly."

"It felt like I had been gone for years." Uri bowed his head.

"Anyway, it will take a long time for this village to heal. There is much joy and much sorrow. Everyone knows that this was all because of Zekod. If his family should ever show up here, I'm afraid they would be stoned to death."

Uri nodded.

Elajon hesitated before he spoke. "I imagine you have a lot to tell. The council will be calling for you to give your testimony in the next few days."

Uri took a deep breath, trying to control all the emotions flooding his mind. "I have a feeling mine might be slightly different than Oden's. I pray he doesn't get carried away and embellish his story too much."

"Oden knows when to control himself. He might try to impress others, but when it counts, he will be truthful."

"Your breakfast is ready." Marga called.

***

Early the next morning Uri got out of bed and went into the kitchen. He washed his face and opened the back door. Outside the air was cool and refreshing. The night had been full of terrors, and his dreams continued until dawn. He couldn't recall them, however he still felt the fear and pain they produced.

The sun felt warm and relaxing on his face. He listened to the familiar sound of the Dombara village awakening to the new day and felt the tensions of the night ebb away.

He went to the coup and stood among the ovis. They came up to him, expecting food. He went to the feedbags and sprinkled seed over the ground. Excited, they scurried about, clucking and eating.

"It doesn't take much to make you guys happy." His spirits began to lift.

Uri went to the nests and began to look for the eggs.

"Whatcha doing?"

Uri recognized Bibbi's voice. "What are you doing out of bed?"

"Oh, I feel fine." Bibbi began to help Uri. "I wanted some fresh air."

"I am happy you are feeling so good." Uri tussled his brother's hair.

"Did you find Zekod?" Bibbi asked.

"Yes, we found him."

"Did you bring him back?"

"No, he was killed." Uri knew because of Bibbi's intense curiosity, he would not stop asking questions.

"Killed, how? Did you kill him?"

Uri opened up and told him the truth. "No, Oden did. He saved my life. Zekod was about to kill me. He and Rill were behind this whole thing."

"How did Oden kill him?"

"Gosh, Bibbi do you really want to know all the grizzly details?" Uri asked.

"Yes."

"Okay, just don't tell Father I told you. Zekod was coming at me. His face was the picture of intense anger. He was going to strangle me with his bare hands. Rill was holding me, so I couldn't defend myself. Suddenly, Oden came up behind him and stabbed him in the back. Zekod fell dead at my feet. Then the Bast came and arrested me. They planned to kill me. That was when Luwanna showed up and saved my life."

Bibbi hung on every word, his eyes wide, and his face coming closer to Uri as he spoke. Then he grabbed on to Uri and hugged him tightly. "I love you. I am so glad you are safe."

Uri hugged him back. "So am I." He replied. "Today is going to be a busy one. So let's get breakfast going."

They hurried to the hut and into the kitchen with light, happy hearts.

When evening arrived, however, Uri's heart was not so light. He had spent many hours in front of the council, telling his story and answering questions. He felt weary as he stopped to visit Luwanna and told her parents of Rill's obsession in capturing her. Then Uri went to see Jai and Aleeta. No one had told them of Zekod's death, so he gave them the sad news.

They sat on the front steps with Uri. "I have something sad to tell you." he began. "We found Zekod, and by the way Jai, Rill is still alive. He brought me to Zekod. He came at me with murderous thoughts. I think he wanted to strangle me to death. At that moment, Oden came from behind and stabbed him in the back. He died right away."

"Well, I can't say I feel any grief." Jai said. "I am surprised about Rill, though."

Aleeta wiped her face. "He was so mean. I don't know why I am crying over him."

Uri took her hand in his. "After all, he was your father. I am sure you feel many emotions concerning him."

"He wasn't always mean and cruel. I have good memories of him when I was very young."

"Hang on to those." Uri said.

It was both a relief and a tragedy. Now Aleeta could safely begin her new life, and it was late when Uri left to go home. The day had been full of emotion. He thankfully returned at dinnertime, relieved this day was over. All he wanted to do was have dinner and be with his family. He soon would have to leave for Pinola Land to prepare for his last year at school.

As Uri stepped into the house, Coran came from the kitchen to greet him. "I stopped by to see you. I'm relieved you're home safe."

"I am glad to be home." Uri answered. "I heard you got your job done. Just about everyone is healthy again."

"We lost a couple." Coran shook his head. "I guess that was to be expected."

"I just came from Aleeta and Jai. I told them about Zekod." Uri said.

"I need to go and see how she is doing." Coran said. "I haven't spent much time with her."

"I am sure she will like that."

They smiled at each other.

Everything had come full circle. The poisonings began with the Pinola tribe. Then Uri traveled to Dombara Land where the poisonings grew worse. Next, he went to the land of the Bast to solve the problem. Now he was back at his Dombara home. Finally, he would go back to Pinola Land where it all began.

After dinner, he excused himself and went to the room he shared with Bibbi. He lay on his bed thinking he would rest for a few moments before going outside to be with the family in the cool of the early evening. In his mind, Uri reviewed all that had taken place in the Bast Land, from beginning of the trip, through meeting Bo and Kee, the capture and his confrontation with the idol. He pondered the way Luwanna had helped them escape, and the trek to the village of the mountain people. Uri thought of the missing women and wondered where they might be, and who took them.

Soon he would have to leave Luwanna and go back to finish school, back to Pinola Land where it all began. He tried to lay plans for the future. However, the exhaustion gave way to a deep, restless sleep. Tomorrow would have to take care of itself.

GLOSSARY
FOR THE URI CHRONICLES   1 AND 2

Key-   MT – Mark of the Tattoo   DO- The Dengu Odyssey
        P – Pinola   D – Dombara
        MP – Mountain People   B - Bast

PEOPLE

CHARACTER	INTRODUCED IN	WHO THEY ARE
Abosol; **ab**-o-sol	DO	D - friend
Ajaban; **a**-ja-ben	DO	Dombara doctor
Aleeta; a-**leet**-a	DO	P - Zekod's daughter
Ambora; am-**bor**-a	DO	P - Zekod's wife- Aleeta's mother
Ando; **an**-do	MT	D - Jai's father –leader
Beason; **bee**-son	MT	D – killer of the getiru
Beka; **bek**-a	MT	P – Uri's Pinola sister
Bibbi **bib**-ee	MT	D – Uri's brother
Bo; **bo**	DO	Bast – Kee's brother
Capel ca-**pel**	DO	D-Village carpenter
Cherka; **cher**-ka	MT	D - Jai's sister
Coran; Coo-**rain**	MT	D- Uri's cousin and priest
Darv; **darv**	DO	D – Luwanna's baby brother
Denar; den-**ar**	MT	P- Uri's first convert
Denola; den-**o**-la	MT	D – Pujim's wife
Dree; dr-**ee**	DO	D - Rill's friend
Dron; **dron**	MT	D - Rill's friend
Elajon; **el**-a-jon	MT	D – Uri and Bibbi's father
Elari; el-**are**-ee	DO	D – Head priest
Frash; **frash**	MT	D – Jai's younger brother
Ferra; fer-**ra**	DO	D – Jai's Dombara mother
Fewbin; **few**-bin	DO	P – Zekod's buddy
Gradis; **gra**-dis	DO	D –priest in Pinola Land
Goth; **goth**	MT	D – Jai's older Brother
Jai; **jay**-eye	MT	D – Uri's friend
Jinela; jin-**el**-a	DO	D musician
Kee; **key**	DO	Bast – young boy
Kerka; **ker**-ka	MT	D – aka Luwanna
Kinter; **kint**-er	DO	D – Coran's father
Koori; koo-**ri**	MT	D – Tika's husband, priest
Kwoll; **kwoll**	DO	P – poisoned man
Letura; le-**tu**-ra	DO	D - poisoned woman

217

Lilla; **lil**-la	DO	P – Kwoll's wife
Luwanna; lu-**wan**-na	MT	D – aka Kerka
Lyshon; **ly**-shon	DO	D – Luwanna's sister
Marga; **mar**-ga	MT	D – Uri's mother
Miltas; **milt**-as	DO	P – Zekod's friend
Mordan; **mor**-dan	MT	D – Priest, Coran's friend
Niliab; **nil**-e-ab	MT	D – Uri's Dombara name
Oden; **o**-den	DO	Dombara/Mudan – half breed
Pattis; **pat**-tis	MT	P – Chief
Pelli; pel-**ee**	DO	Mountain People- Kee's friend
Pishob; **pish**-ob	MT	P – Zekod's Older son
Pujim; **pu**-jim	MT	D - Chief
Ranui; ra-**nu**-ee	DO	D – Tika and Koori's baby
Rill; **rill**	MT	D – Uri's adversary
Sarella ; sar-**el**-la	MT	D – Uri's sister
Solari; sol-**air**-ee	DO	Mountain People – Vakier's wife
Suwat; **su**-wat	MT	P – Beka's husband
Tareen ; tar-**een**	MT	D – Luwanna's friend
Tau; **tau**	DO	Bast - Priest
Tika; **tea**-kah	MT	D – Uri's older sister
Tofini; to-**feen**-ee	DO	P – A man that was poisoned
Turik; **tu**-rik	MT	P – Zekod's son
Uri; **ur**-i (not **your**-ee)	MT	D – lead
Vakier; **vak**-ear	DO	Mountain People - chief
Zekod; **zek**-odd	MT	P –Jai's Pinola father

ANIMALS

NAME	INTRODUCED IN	DESCRIPTION
Bamea **ba**-mea	MT	Sheep-like
Black Eel **eel**	DO	Poisonous river eel
Chola **cho**-la	DO	Lizard
Ebor **ee**-bor	DO	Black Beast
Gaunat **gwon**-at	DO	Bat-like
Getiru get-**ir**-oo	MT	large tiger-like animal
hoperl hop-**pearl**	DO	prey, rat-like with rabbit ears
Kavak kav-**ack**	MT	Goat-like
Keymon **kei**-mon	DO	Tree climber with a long tail- medium size
Noogan **noo**-gan	MT	Beast of burden donkey-size
Outnu **out**-nu	DO	Large prey animal, antlers deer-like
Ovi **o**-vee	MT	chicken-like birds
Slopboer **slop**-boer	DO	Magget-like worms, dig holes

			in the ground
Wona	**wo**-na	MT	Worm in the desert sand 3-4 feet long

VEGETATION

NAME		INTRODUCED IN	DESCRIPTION
Blowplant;	**blow**-plant	DO	A stong smelling weed
Cheekee fruit;	**chee**-kee	DO	A fruit that grows in the Bast area
Dengu Plant;	**den**-gu	DO	The Queen of the Forest in the Bast area
Meechu Tree;	**me**-chew	DO	A tree-poison made from boiling it's twigs in water
Osis;	**o**-sis	DO	A narcotic made from the root of the Osis plant
Piutti tree;	**piu**-tee	DO	A tree that has pain killing properties
Porgour ;	por-**gour**	DO	A material made from the Dengu leaves
Tangleroot;	**tan**-gle-root	MT	A tree grown in Bast area
Tobanyant;	toe-**ban**-yant	MT	A low growing tree with rich fruit

GEOGRAPHY and PEOPLE

DOMBARA CONTINENT
Bast Tribe; **ba**ast
Dombara Land; **dome**-bar-a
Dombara Tribe
Mountain People
Mudan Tribe; mu-**dan**

WATERWAYS
Bast River
Dombara River
Green Sea
Jocoo Bay; **joe**-coo
Mudan River
Nui River; new-**ee**
Pic River
Shai River; **shy**
Sho River; **show**
Tol River; **toll**

PIUCHA CONTINENT

Brown Hills
Pinola Land; pin-**o**-la
Pinola Tribe
Rabir Tribe; ray-**beer**

WATERWAYS
Green Sea

219

Valley of the Caves
Yoka Tribe;   **yo**-ka

MISCELLANEOUS

Crost; **crowst**	hot drink made from beans
Cussel; **cuss**-el	a wooden board and pebbles
Shoo Rites; **shoe**	coming of age Bast rites for males
Slether; **sle**-ther	a Mudan sling type weapon
Talisman; **tal** is-man	a scarecrow structure made for scaring away Evil Spirits

www.ingramcontent.com/pod-product-compliance
Lightning Source LLC
Chambersburg PA
CBHW071328250626
47159CB00004B/1504